D0700620

MODERN METAMORPHOSES

MODERN METAMORPHOSES

STORIES OF TRANSFORMATION

CORNELIA FEYE, EDITOR

KONSTELLATION PRESS

Published by

Konstellation Press, San Diego

www.konstellationpress.com

Copyright © 2020 by Cornelia Feye, editor

All rights reserved.

No part of this book may be reproduced in any form or by any electronic or mechanical means, including information storage and retrieval systems, without written permission from the author, except for the use of brief quotations in a book review.

Copy-editor: Lisa Wolff

Coverdesign: Sebastian Feye

Editor: Cornelia Feye

FOREWORD

"I intend to speak of forms changed into new entities." Ovid

In life as in art, transformation is unavoidable. We change, the world around us changes, and the people things and animals we love change as well. The twelve authors of the 2nd Friday Writers have populated their stories with characters that transform into animals, monsters, zombies, vampires, ghosts, or simply into better human beings.

For two years, we have read, edited, questioned and improved each other's stories during our monthly meetings at the Point Loma Hervey Library. The 2nd Friday writers follow in the footsteps of the 2nd Thursday Writers anthology *Magic. Mystery & Murder,* which won the San Diego Book Award in 2019.

We want to thank Writers Ink in Liberty Station for the Short Story classes, which provided many of our authors with the tools to express themselves. We also want to thank the Point Loma library for hosting us. And finally we would like to thank Sebastian Feye for the transformative cover art alphabet.

We thank our readers for taking the time to read our stories. We enjoyed the process, and it was transformative for us as well. If we can't stop change, we might as well have fun with it.

Cornelia Feye
    San Diego, March 20, 2020

CONTENTS

LITTLE RED DOT - VALERIE HANSEN

I'm not a serial killer. Far from it. But seven months ago I was reading my AARP magazine and I saw this tiny ad in the back: "Meth Lab Neighbors? Rude Bank Teller? Get rid of any thorn in your side. Laser Gun. Guaranteed to vaporize the peskiest people within 24 hours of a 'hit'. Money Back Guarantee. Only $499.99. lasergun.com."

I was intrigued. I mean, who doesn't have *someone* they'd love to annihilate? I didn't have $500 just lying around, but I could scrape it up. I'd worked for thirty-five years as a registered nurse. My late husband had been an engineer at General Dynamics before that bastard William Anders—I don't care if he was an Apollo 8 astronaut—broke it up and sold it off piece by piece in the nineties. We were always careful to save as much as we could.

I got on the World Wide Web and looked up that laser gun company. There all these testimonials from satisfied customers. All you had to do was aim the gun at the person who was bugging you, push the button, see a red dot appear anywhere on their body, and leave the scene. At some random point between thirty minutes and twenty-four hours later—

when you were long gone—the "target" would miraculously vaporize, leaving nary a trace. What did I have to lose?

The only reason I could even use the Internet was my daughter, Corina. She insisted we buy her a home computer when they first came out and she learned how to use it in no time. When they started that World Wide Web, she jumped on it, even though it took about ten minutes to connect to a site in those days. She taught me everything I know about computers.

The laser arrived in a little brown box about four days after I ordered it. It looked like a garage door fob. Just a two-inch black rectangle with a button on top and a small opening on the end.

Now I don't know about you, but I practically need an interpreter to read the instruction manuals that come with gadgets these days. It definitely wasn't written by an American: "Laser clean itself. Simple wipe soft cloth, if soiled. Will deactivate if submersion in liquid."

But I got the gist of it. Best thing I read was you don't even have to take the fob out of your pocket. It will fire right through your clothes and doesn't do any damage to them at all! Doesn't even harm the clothes of your "target."

About a year ago my daughter told me I had to lose ten pounds. Easier said than done. I would have ignored her, except she's also my doctor. She told me to try walking. So I'm taking two long walks a day—downtown—where I live in San Diego.

I slipped that little laser into my pocket and set out on my morning walk. I like to go out early, before breakfast, around seven o'clock. I wasn't planning to kill anyone that morning, but I wanted to be prepared if I saw something I didn't like. Besides, I wanted to see if it even worked.

There are a lot of homeless people moving around that time of day—rifling through the trash, looking for things they can recycle. One guy was taking everything out of a trash can and dropping it on the ground. A row of tents blocked most of the sidewalk on 8th between F and E. I try to avoid those encampments, because they're always so smelly. There was a man in dirty gray clothes pissing against a recessed doorway near 7th and F Street.

I walked toward 4th, so I could buy a coffee at Starbucks in Horton Plaza. That tides me over until I get home and fix breakfast. A woman sat on a pile of bedding inside one of those fenced-off outdoor eating areas most of the local restaurants have. Her hair was scraggly and she wasn't wearing a top—bare boobs exposed to the whole neighborhood. But what bothered me the most was the huge pile of trash, like a moat, surrounding her.

I knew there was no way she'd clean it up when she moved on. The afflicted and the addicted never bother to pick up the cardboard they've been sleeping on. Sometimes they don't even pick up their stained sleeping bags—probably figure some do-gooder church group will provide a clean one the next night anyway.

I think, "Perfect. Let's test this baby out."

I discreetly angled the fob in my pocket, pointed it in her direction, and pushed the button. I saw a little red dot of light appear on her shoulder. I released the trigger and went on my merry way.

Next morning, I walked the same way and there was no sign of her or the trash.

"Nice," I said to myself.

About a week later, I was taking my afternoon walk—by the way, I've lost five pounds so far—around Seaport Village. I moved along at my normal brisk pace—not bad for a seventy-nine-year-old—when I saw a man walking his golden retriever.

Now don't get me wrong—I love dogs. I would never do anything to hurt a dog. But I hate the lazy owners who won't scoop their dog's poop. And there are a lot of them downtown. The retriever did his business, right on the sidewalk, and the owner ignored it—just walked away. Exasperated, I fired that sweet little red beam right into the middle of the man's back.

I got my new AARP magazine around that time. I read it while I ate my lunch. When I got to the very back, where all those little ads are, I noticed the laser gun ad wasn't there anymore. No biggie; I still had the web address. But when I tried logging on to the website, my computer said: "Safari Can't Find Server."

I dug the instruction book out of my file cabinet, only to discover there wasn't an address or phone number listed anywhere. It wouldn't have minded, but what if the gun stopped working and I needed to order another one?

I started thinking I'd better preserve this little baby, not use it up. But a few days later one of those obnoxious teenagers on an electric scooter whizzed by me at fifteen miles per hour right on the sidewalk and scared the bejesus out of me. Damn, I hate those things. You can't hear them coming and, I swear, those kids get as close as they possibly can, using pedestrians as slalom gates.

Got him right in the back of the head, even though he was half a block away by the time I recovered my wits enough to aim.

I wasn't feeling one bit guilty about vaporizing at that point. As far as I was concerned, there are too many people in this city as it is. But I *was* wondering if the laser even worked. I mean, how do I know these scumbags are actually gone? I don't see them disappear right when I shoot them.

Reading the paper a few weeks later, I saw a tiny article on page A11: "Mysterious Disappearances Unexplained—Officials in Multiple Communities Baffled." Turned out there'd been vaporizing all over. Eyewitnesses said people were there one second and gone the next, leaving a pile of clothing and nothing else.

Apparently it was working. There was lots of speculation in the article. Some skeptics claimed the eyewitnesses were crazy. But there'd been so many reports, from all over the country, that various law enforcement agencies were investigating.

As the months went by, there were more and more articles in the paper, on the TV news, and on talk radio. No one could figure out what was going on. No one thought it was the

Rapture, 'cause none of the victims was that good of a person. In fact, according to reports, it was primarily shady politicians—wish I'd thought of them—registered child molesters, and just plain mean, ornery people vanishing.

That led me to thinking. It was great that I'd been cleaning up the streets of my neighborhood. The homeless population was plummeting. Word on the street was: If you're living out here, your odds of getting vaporized are high. But what about people I knew personally?

My son-in-law, Darrel, to be exact. Okay, he's not a criminal. But Corina's worked her butt off all her life. She put herself through college on scholarships and work-study grants, she borrowed money for med school—and paid every cent off early —she practically stayed awake 24/7 for a whole year of internship, and she slept at the hospital on a hard little cot in a claustrophobic closet for three years of residency. Then what did she do? She married this loser who hasn't held a steady job their entire married life.

Sure, Darrel worked for short periods. But the pay wasn't good enough, the commute was too long, the boss was impossible—you name it, he had an excuse to quit. He'd been living off Corina for over twenty years. I was sick and tired of it. Nothing burned me up more than going over to their house and watch her come dragging in after a long, hard day of work, only to start cooking dinner for the lot of us. That bastard didn't lift a finger. He said he didn't know how to cook. Apparently he didn't know how to do the dishes either. But he had no problem calling up a bunch of his friends to come over and eat with us.

Darrel never fixed anything around the house, didn't do a lick of yard or housework— Corina did it all herself before she could afford to hire a gardener and a cleaning service. Not only that, but he drank. And he was a sloppy, maudlin drunk. I couldn't stand him. My late husband didn't like him either. Called him "the prima donna."

Of course my grandsons thought he was funny—he always had them laughing until they cried. And he took Corina dancing when they were younger. But what good was that? It didn't put food on the table or keep a roof over their heads. I figured Corina hadn't divorced him because it was too much trouble. Well, now I had the means of eliminating him without any trouble at all.

He went out to breakfast every morning. So I drove up to Carmel Valley, where they live, and parked close to the entrance of his favorite little restaurant. I sat there, waiting, until he finally strolled past my car. I "beamed" him real quick, before he got in the door. Then I headed home, pleased with my day's work.

Corina called me in hysterics that night, about seven thirty. Said she'd just gotten home from work and there was a pile of clothes in his recliner, but Darrel was nowhere to be seen. She thought he'd been vaporized. Why would anyone want to hurt her husband, she wanted to know. A kinder, gentler man never existed. I tried to console her and tell her I'd be right over, but inside I was doing a little dance. Good riddance!

When I got to Corina's house, both my grandsons and a couple of policewomen were there with her. Corina told them what she could, but she wasn't at home when it happened, so she really didn't know anything. And no one has figured out what causes these vaporizations, so there really wasn't anything the police could do except file the report. My daughter was distraught and even my grandsons were crying—and that bastard never took the time to go to any of their soccer games when they were growing up.

~

I figured once the initial shock had worn off, the memorial service was endured, and a little time had passed, my daughter and grandsons would get on with their lives. But months later, after they'd all gone back to work, everyone still seemed really depressed. Corina was too thin—her clothes were hanging on her. I went over one Saturday afternoon and her eyes were red and puffy. She told me that she was lost without Darrel. She came home from work and there wasn't anyone to talk to—my grandsons had returned to their own apartments. There wasn't anyone to make her laugh or give her a massage.

He gave her massages? Who knew? But now she wouldn't have to share any of her retirement money. She was still attractive. She could meet a nice, hardworking man who actually supported her, someone who liked to cook, a man who would travel with her—Darrel hated to go anywhere new.

Of course, I kept my mouth shut. Even began to wonder if I'd done the right thing. I didn't like Darrel, but it looked like my daughter really loved that alcoholic—hard as it was to believe. And my grandsons were just as bad. The oldest was so depressed about losing his dad that he had to go on medication. The younger one started having terrible anxiety attacks— wondering who would disappear next.

A lot of people were having anxiety about that. It had become a mental health epidemic, according to a psychiatrist I heard on the news. I noticed everyone scrutinizing the people around them, like secret service agents, everywhere I went. In fact, I wasn't seeing that many people out and about anymore. More people were shopping online and working from home. No one wanted to go out in public. I heard just the other day that the suicide rate was spiraling out of control.

I was beginning to regret I'd ever bought the gun. I thought maybe I should take a hammer to that little fob—dispose of the pieces in as many trash cans around town as I could. But part of me was reluctant to give it up.

Earlier today I was on my way to Costco and I accidentally cut off a pedestrian crossing G at 8th. I never even noticed her as I tried to make my right turn against the red light. Luckily, she jumped back in time. I slammed on my brakes and said "sorry" through my windshield. She just glared. When I glanced down to see if my cell phone had slid off the passenger seat, I noticed a little red dot on my right breast.

2

THE THIRD RING - V.A.CHRISTIE

Maura Sutter always answered on the third ring.

"We have your granddaughter," a man told her. "Chloe."

"What?" Maura asked.

"The ransom is twenty thousand. No negotiations. No police. You will be contacted with further instructions in five minutes."

"I want to speak to—"

"No," the man said.

The phone went dead in her hand.

Maura dialed frantically.

Chloe did not pick up. Not unusual. For her, anyway.

Maura dug through her drawer for Facebook information. She sent a message to Chloe's account, and held her breath.

The phone rang again and she answered it.

"You will send a MoneyGram," the man told her. "The Vons on Mayfair. Do you know how to get there?"

"Yes," she said.

"The account number will be texted to your phone. Failure to follow instructions will lead to your granddaughter's death."

Maura's phone made a farting sound. She read the number

on the screen. The phone made another fart and directions appeared.

~

A car swerved into her lane to avoid a bicyclist and Maura slammed on the brake. Light-headed, she parked by the side of the road.

Maura gulped air, as her heart raced. *It's OK*, she told herself, *it's OK*. She would be no good to anyone if she had a heart attack.

She reached into her purse and extracted her phone.

One missed call and a message, the phone informed her.

She entered the password and listened to the message.

"Mother. I do not understand your message. Chloe is at school. Where else would she be? Call me back. Or I will come over."

That, Maura thought would be all she needed. A visit from her daughter, Janet, was like a military inspection, minus any warmth or understanding.

Hands shaking, Maura turned on her laptop and used the instructions Chloe had given her to log on to Facebook.

"What is wrong?" Chloe's message read.

Six minutes had passed since the message was sent.

"Where are you?" Maura wrote.

"Class," Chloe wrote back. "U OK? Expect a visit from The Mother, btw."

"Send me a photo of yourself," Maura wrote.

"Why?" Chloe wrote.

"It's important," Maura wrote.

"I can't. Class."

"Please," Maura wrote.

"Fine," Chloe wrote. "Give me a couple minutes."

Her granddaughter logged off.

Maura took a deep breath. The people who contacted her had offered no proof. She had no proof, though, that Chloe was where she said she was.

Maura turned the engine back on and continued toward the Vons.

The phone buzzed again and Maura answered it.

"Mother," the voice said. "I am at your house. Where are you?"

"I'm going to the Vons on Mayfair," Maura said. "Have you heard from Chloe?"

"Yes," Janet said. "Are you driving? Right now? And you answered the phone? Put it on speaker."

"There's no time for that now," Maura said, not wanting to explain that she could not recall how to accomplish Janet's command. "I'm almost there. And I am a perfectly fine driver. Of the two of us, who has had three accidents, five tickets, and two parking tickets?"

"Mother," Janet said, "I left work to check on you. When you come back—"

"I was contacted by people who claimed to have kidnapped Chloe. But I think it's a cyber-kidnapping. I heard about it on the news."

"There is no such thing as cyber-kidnapping. I'm on my way," Janet announced and hung up the phone.

Her daughter was like LBJ. As soon as she had the information she wanted, or didn't want, she had no further use for the conversation. And judging by her final comment, Janet was on her way, driving like a bat out of hell no doubt.

Maura parked the car and checked Facebook again.

Chloe had sent a photo of herself surrounded by classmates and a disgruntled-looking professor. The board behind them showed the date, and the clock showed two minutes had passed since the photo had been taken.

"Chloe," she wrote into the messenger.

"Yes?"

"I love you."

"Love you too, grandma."

Maura looked around the parking lot. No one looked suspicious, as far as she could tell.

Her daughter wanted to take away her car and stop her from driving, never mind that she could pass all her tests, hadn't had so much as fender-bender, and never got lost.

Get gray hair and some wrinkles and everyone thought you were mentally handicapped. She looked around. Everyone from the chubby children to their harried parents was going to get old, if they were lucky, but none of them had any consideration or respect for anyone who earned their age.

She considered going back home; instead she stepped into the damp afternoon.

~

Maura walked into the store and up to the customer service counter.

"I would like to send a MoneyGram," she told the clerk.

The clerk stole a quick glance at her rings.

"You have the number you want to send the payment to?" she asked.

"Yes," Maura said, looking around.

She was beginning to wonder if her plan was a good idea. In fact she was pretty sure it was not, but it was too late to back out now.

"And it is?" the clerk asked in a bored tone.

"Can the money I send be tracked?" Maura asked.

"Um," the young woman said, "MoneyGram is a secure way in which to send money from person to person . . . but if you are uncertain of the number it would be better to check before you send anything."

A man approached them. He looked utterly unremarkable. Just a middle-aged man, slim but for his belly, with bad skin, glasses, and a pronounced widow's peak.

"Hi," the man said. "Can I help?"

The voice on her phone had been altered, but something in

the pitch and tone made Maura nearly certain this stranger was the man whose voice had threatened her granddaughter.

"Let me get my manager—"

"Oh, there's no need for that," the man said. "I'm Maura's neighbor. I'll just help. If that's alright."

Maura faked a smile. "Thank you so much. I'm so confused. It's my granddaughter."

"Oh," the clerk said. "You are sending money to your granddaughter. I'll be right back."

"Don't worry about that," the man said. "Everything's fine. Janet is going to be fine."

"Chloe." Maura sniffed, fishing Kleenex from her purse. She could not actually manage fake tears, but the Kleenex helped give the impression.

"Right," the man said. "I get them confused. You know . . . it was the barbecue, right?"

Barbecue? Maura thought, wondering if she had ever encountered this man in any previous capacity. Well, the statement sounded neighborly, and that was what he was pretending to be.

"Excuse me," the manager said.

She knew him. Vaguely. And he knew her as well. Vaguely.

The man looked nervous. "Maura is my neighbor. I'm just helping her send some money to her . . ." The man consulted his phone briefly. "Granddaughter."

"I will take over from here," the manager said. "Thank you for your help."

"Maura is confused," the man said. "I am just trying to help her."

"You know what?" the manager said. "I have seen Maura many times. And I've yet to see her confused about anything. You, on the other hand, I have never laid eyes on before."

"Look. I was only trying to help," the man whined.

He turned and headed toward the exit, inspecting his phone as he went.

"Orhan," Maura said after a quick scan of the manager's name tag. "That man is part of a . . . scam."

She pulled out her phone and showed Orhan the messages. A new one appeared as the man walked away.

"You are putting your granddaughter in danger. Maura. You have five minutes to comply. You are responsible for Chloe's life," the message read. Knowing it was false did nothing to halt the squeeze of anxiety that hit her heart when she read it.

Orhan took a quick look and ran after the man. The man looked back and tripped on a stack of plastic shopping baskets near the door.

"Sir," Orhan said sarcastically to the man sprawled on the floor with the automatic door shuddering open and closed every few seconds. "I am going to have to ask you to come with me."

∼

"Good thing you watch the news, Mom," Janet told her as the news came on. "Though I must say, this gang has to be on the Least Competent Criminals list. I mean, going in person?"

"And how would you have done it?" Maura asked.

"Not in person, I can assure you," Janet answered. "We are going to have to work on your Internet settings. So this—"

"Shh," Maura told her.

"My God," Janet said. "The only thing keeping that woman's blouse on is fate."

"Janet," Maura said. "Shh."

"This afternoon some local thieves messed with the wrong grandma," the news lady informed the audience.

"My," Janet said when the camera shifted to Orhan. "You should have told me the manager was so . . ." She trailed off and swallowed some merlot. "Hmm. Attractive. Maybe I'll switch Vons."

The story concluded with a warning about thieves and scams and those who targeted the elderly.

"Just call me Action Grandma," Maura said. "I think I should be played by Helen Mirren."

Janet laughed and poured them each another glass of wine.

3

THE BLUE RECLINER - LINA KAROLINE CASTILLO

Based on True Events

D aniel and Grandma Rose shared a strong and special bond. It wasn't just that they shared the same birthday, born forty-five years apart. It was what they had endured. On today's birthday they had much to celebrate. Daniel had been taking his meds so regularly that he didn't hear the voices anymore—the angels and the demons, his counselor called them. Daniel, looking fit and trim and wearing the new flowered aloha shirt that Grandma Rose got him, was eager to see how many of his sisters, cousins, and their families would come. It was Saturday, June 16, 2012. He was forty years old.

From his spot on the front couch, Daniel watched the cars come up Komo Mai Drive. His favorite cousin, Will, and his son pulled up in front of the house.

Daniel walked into the kitchen, where Aunty Bea was helping Grandma Rose take the kalua pig out of the oven. "Boy, that smells good." Grabbing a bite from the pot, Daniel turned to leave. "Yum, so 'ono! Will's here—I'm going down to help him bring up some boxes."

Grandma Rose smiled at him and nodded.

"He's doing so well, Rose." Aunty Bea's face flushed from the steam rising over the pig. "It's been so hard on you, all these years."

Grandma Rose looked into the eyes of her youngest sister and best friend. "He's my special boy. Can we please not go there today? Let's just have a good time. Okay?"

After the food, the fun, and the birthday cake, it was time for presents. Daniel's three sisters, cousin Will, and their families mingled around the kitchen and adjoining family room, the little ones still munching on coconut haupia cake and running all over the place. Daniel beamed, surrounded by love. He opened the box from Will and his eyes grew wide.

"Sorry it's a hand-me-down," Will said. "I got a new Xbox for Junior, and he suggested we give this one to you. It has a ton of games on it, and I remember the fun we used to have playing…"

"No violent games, right?" Aunty Bea's eyes narrowed. "The doctor said he can't watch those."

"No, we cleaned the console out. But there's a bunch of fun ones, like Minecraft, Junior's favorite." He patted his son's shoulder.

Everyone watched as Aunty Bea lifted the flannel sheet from the hulking present in the middle of the family room with the big blue ribbon on top. It was the recliner Grandma Rose been admiring at Sears Roebuck for months. Her hand touched her mouth, but she couldn't suppress the smile. "How did you know?"

"Daniel told us, and we all chipped in."

Daniel's jaw lowered, and his brown eyes looked into his grandmother's. "You like it, right, Grandma?"

"Oh, I love it, and it's my favorite color." She walked over to give him a hug, then settled into the recliner, patting the light blue Naugahyde. The family broke into a chorus of "Happy Birthday."

~

The angels touched him on his shoulder and whispered, "You took care of each other." They were the welcomed whispers. Not like the others. Daniel could feel the angels' soft, moist breath. He struggled to hear them. Blood pulsed through his head.

"She loved you," the angel voices sang in unison. "You were her special boy."

"Special." Daniel's mind flashed back to grade school. Not like "special" meant when you had to go to Mrs. Akana's class. The other kids, the ones that were not special, would corner him in the playground and called him dumb. Dunce. Mental. Slow. Retard.

"She loved you and took care of you." The angels' voices rose like a church choir.

Daniel remembered. He was nine when his mother left and moved to California.

"Momma didn't want me."

But Grandma Rose did, and she never gave up on him. So many doctors for so many years. She took him for treatment, and test after test after test. Back to the doctor's they went when the medicine didn't work and gave him headaches instead. Even when, on his twenty-sixth birthday, the voices in his head started talking and Dr. Chen diagnosed schizophrenia, she didn't give up.

The years passed. His sisters married and moved on. Only he and Grandma Rose remained.

"You tried so hard to get better, Daniel, and you did," the angels told him. "Think of the good times."

He remembered taking Grandma Rose to the doctor's and the trips they made each week to Queen's Hospital in Honolulu for her arthritis. Then the long drive over the winding Pali Highway to the windward side of Oahu, where Aunty Bea was waiting. Daniel drove the two elderly sisters to Kin Sun Restaurant, overlooking Kaneohe Bay. Over a lunch of Crispy Gau Gee, steamed vegetables, and saimin noodle soup, the women would laugh and cry and tell Daniel about the crazy things they used to do when they were young.

"You watched over her," the angels whispered.

Each night, Daniel looked down from the small apartment they had built for him on the hill behind Grandma Rose's house. She would turn the light on the back porch off, signaling that she was okay and going to bed.

Then Daniel returned to his computer and played Mortal Kombat all night long.

Grandma Rose didn't know about the game, even though it was she who suggested they go to the Kam Swap Meet, where he wandered off to the video game booth as she picked through the papayas at the fruit stand. The know-it-all boy spied Daniel looking through the action games and pulled one from the pile. "Hey, Bro, you can stop looking. This one's the best." He handed Daniel the Mortal Kombat Komplete Edition. "It's just out, but I can give you a deal."

～

Months later, at twilight, a winter storm kicked the winds up from Manana Valley. Daniel put down the Xbox controls and wiped his scratchy red eyes with his dirty T-shirt. He tried to focus on the trees swaying outside the window. The rain raked the garden below, the broken fence swaying in the breeze. Why hadn't he finished mending the fence and put away the hammer that now lay in the rain on the workbench? Why was Grandma's porch light still on?

He couldn't remember the last time he had worked in the garden, or talked to Grandma Rose. Daniel had been playing Mortal Kombat for thirty-two hours straight. Hadn't taken his meds in weeks.

From the window overlooking the garden and Grandma Rose's house, he saw shadows—or was it a person?—running through the grass. No, it was Shao Kahn, emperor of Outworld. Daniel remembered watching Shao Kahn bash his opponent's head in with his trademark giant hammer. But what was Shao

Kahn doing outside of the computer, in Grandma Rose's backyard?

If he got in the house, he could hurt Grandma Rose.

Pacing the small, constricted apartment, Daniel lifted his hands to his head and rubbed his brow. Demon voices roared within. He remembered how Goro beat Shao Kahn by using his monstrous fists. Beads of sweat dripped on his forehead. His arms tingled; he punched one hand into the other.

Daniel looked down at his body. He had four arms, each with three thick fingers. His muscles flexed; he was huge. He turned and caught his reflection in the hall mirror. It was Goro. He was Goro, the bronze, four-armed half-human, half-dragon. His fists clenched with anger as he swung open the door and ran down the steps to Grandma Rose's. He raced through the garden, with no sign of Shao Kahn. Outside her door, he grabbed the hammer lying on the workbench and roared. He would defeat Shao Kahn using his own favorite weapon.

Through the back door, Daniel saw Shao Kahn on Grandma Rose's blue recliner.

"Are you all right, dear?" the figure murmured.

～

Demons don't whisper. They yell.

They yelled at Daniel now. "Look at your bloody fist!"

In the bright kitchen light, Daniel squinted at his right hand, bruised and smeared with blood. Blood all over his dirty white T-shirt, blood on the floor, blood on the walls, and blood on the blue recliner that Grandma Rose slumped in. His right hand throbbed.

"Her face!" the demons screamed. "Look at her face!"

Daniel pressed his bloody hands to his ears. Then, eyes wide, he obeyed.

The midnight-colored eyes of Grandma Rose were beaten shut. Her face and head bashed. Blood oozed from the blows and matted her hair, her body limp, shriveled, and sunk low in the blue recliner she loved. Blood covered her blue-and-yellow flowered housedress. The bloodied hammer lay on the floor, like the ending scene of a Mortal Kombat battle.

From the TV on the kitchen counter, Daniel heard the tinkering noise as the wheel turned on Grandma Rose's favorite show. The room stopped spinning; the oxygen was sucked out of it. Even the angels were quiet. His mind cleared. He studied the scene before him.

Tears pouring from his eyes, Daniel stumbled to the kitchen counter, wiped his bloody hands on his jeans, and pulled the cell phone out of Grandma Rose's purse. He dialed 911, just like she had taught him so many years ago.

4

FLOAT - TINA CHILDERS

E mma hadn't been in her backyard since she had her dog Rusty euthanized three months ago. She sat and avoided looking at the holes that Rusty had joyfully dug. June gloom ruled the day. She texted her son Jason.

"Hey how u doing? Did u start your class? How was camping trip?" She started filling the holes and thought about the happy times. Hours later Jason responded.

"Fine. Yes. Good."

Emma smiled to herself. *That's Jason.* She called her husband at work, but he didn't pick up. She texted her other son, Cody, even though a response was unlikely.

"Hi Cody, how's work going?"

Nothing.

Loss blanketed her like the San Diego fog. Their Queensland Heeler had shepherded her through the caregiving and death of her mom. His quiet presence had soothed her when everyone else thought it was time to get over it. Rusty was there when the kids began their own lives. Now, Rusty was dead. And her husband was buried in work.

It dawned on Emma that she was free for the first time in

twenty years. She could take a solo tropical beach vacation. She could float on gentle waves, drink frothy drinks, and decide what comes next.

Emma googled beach resorts with calm ocean waters for floating.

"Float away with Finaladryl and Eliminate your Carbon Footprint" popped up on her screen. "Fifty percent off on a green burial when purchasing our Float Away package."

Emma gasped. This was not a tropical resort but an assisted suicide "spa."

Facebook distracted her with "friends" who had traveled, acquired various cancers, and become grandparents. Emma moved on to her news feed and read about the effects of sea level rise in Florida, random shootings, and beautiful Indian kids squatting and collecting copper wire in a toxic pile of trash. Emma felt complicit in all of it. She returned to the Finaladryl web page and just out of curiosity, filled out the short application. An automatic e-mail popped up saying she'd been scheduled for today at three o'clock. Her brain bounced between shock, horror, and excitement.

She called her husband again. No answer, so she texted Cody.

"Do you think I was a good mom?" No text came back. Emma decided to just go check out the spa. It was something to do.

The Lyft driver talked while he navigated the congested 805 South.

"I can't believe the traffic is this bad at two thirty. But I'm glad I picked up this ride. I really need the money. I have to send money back to my parents in Syria to rebuild their decimated house."

"That's terrible, but it's nice that you're helping them," Emma responded.

"Syria used to be such a beautiful country, but the fighting has ruined it."

The driver spoke as he exited on El Cajon Boulevard and

accelerated through a red light. They passed salons for blowouts, eyebrows, nails, and eyelashes.

"We're here at your Thai restaurant. Don't walk past that strange-looking spa. There are scary-looking protestors down there. And to think I was a neurologist," he muttered as he drove away.

Once he was out of sight, Emma walked toward the spa with purpose. Her pace quickened as she imagined no more arguments, pain, or disappointment. She sprinted past the silent black-clad protestors holding signs.

"This is NOT the way to heaven." "Stay and FIGHT for the rights of others." "Don't take the EASY way out." "Your friends and family LOVE you." "Jesus died so YOU could live."

Emma thought it would be nice to not know about the maniac in The White House, the climate refugees, or the failed recycling programs. Everyone tried to live ethical lives. Was it ethical to eat a pig who'd never had a chance to play?

Emma's mind raced from the giant plastic blob of plastic growing in the ocean to her ridiculous swim shoes that contributed to it. If she just floated away, there would be one less person to squander precious resources.

Emma entered the spa. Before she could explain that she was just checking it out, the receptionist handed her an exit survey. It took one minute to complete. Yes, she realized what she was doing. No, she was not responsible for the care of another person or animal. No, she was not in debt. She wrote down her perfect high school weight. What did it matter now? She gave them her Visa card information. The cost was a tax write-off! That should make her husband happy.

The receptionist took her survey and smiled blankly while glancing at her phone. *What a job, checking people in so they can kill themselves. I will just check out the ocean room and then . . .* Beads of nervous sweat gathered on her forehead. An exit specialist came and led Emma down a cheerful pastel corridor.

Emma started to feel light-headed. Her body moved slowly, urging her brain to think for a moment. She entered a beautiful room with the requested pictures of beaches from all over the world.

"How's it going?" asked the specialist.

"I'm good," she lied. "Sorry I was a little bit late."

"No worries, especially for you! There will be a small pinch as I insert the IV and you'll be on your way."

Emma shifted nervously. Her heart raced and her hands felt clammy. Part of her wanted to turn and run away, but the temptation to just let go kept growing.

"Have you ever thought of doing this?" she asked the woman.

"Can't, student loans," she responded while checking her Instagram.

"Oh, if you happen to change your mind, just push the red button."

Before Emma could voice her apprehension, there was a small prick in her arm. She started to relax.

"Okay, thank you. The photos are lovely."

"It's all good—'bye." The woman left.

The pictures reminded Emma of the joy she had experienced in the ocean. The memories started with numerous beach outings as a kid with her family and continued to wild days with her teenage friends, swimming through forbidden riptides and jumping off piers. She loved visiting tropical islands in Hawaii, the Caribbean, Thailand, anywhere with warm clear water, alone, with her husband, and then with Jason and Cody. She could picture them swimming in the brilliant water, five shades of blue, after a sea turtle. Their smiles.

Her kids! What would this do to them? Doubt flooded her brain.

Emma had experienced so much joy. It was her turn to give back to the Earth, especially the ocean. Had she gone completely insane? Emma willed her arm to reach for the red button, but it wouldn't move. She tried to yell for help. She pictured her deceased mother rolling her eyes in disapproval—so dramatic.

"Wait," she screamed inside her head, "help me, I'm not ready, PLEASE STOP!"

Her brain began to calm down. A peaceful feeling filled her body as she floated into a deep, dark sleep.

She woke up. There was not supposed to be waking up, so the specialist must have given her the wrong dose! Maybe because she lied about her weight.

How could she have been drawn in by that crazy website? She yanked the IV out of her arm and bolted to the lobby.

"I changed my mind!" she announced. No one looked up from their phones.

A sign on the door said NO REFUNDS. She walked out into the bright sun.

5

CORAL GARDENS - CORNELIA FEYE

Taylor felt the warmth of the fire pit on her back and the cool, salty breeze of the Pacific Ocean on her face.

"This is the sweet spot right between fire and water, heat and cool, night and day," she said to her husband Sean.

He smiled philosophically at his mai tai, glowing orange in the firelight.

Built with local lava stones and recycled wood, the eco-friendly Coral Gardens Resort prided itself on being as self-sustaining as possible. It grew its own pineapples and coffee plants, and avoided using packing material or non-biodegradable decorations, such as paper umbrellas in the happy hour cocktails. Sean and Taylor had come here for the restored coral reef and for the beauty of Kaanapali Beach, where the trade winds gently tousled the palm fronds like the hair of a beloved child.

"I can't wait to see the reef tomorrow," Taylor said, as she took a sip of her piña colada cocktail, mixed with local pineapple and coconuts. "Remember a few years ago when this was still the Black Rock Inn, and the entire reef was bleached white? There was no color left and no fish," she reminisced.

Sean nodded. "That's what global warming and mass tourism will do to the corals."

The surf at the beach glittered in the rising moonlight, when the soothing sound of the waves crashing onto sand was interrupted by an angry voice.

"Leave me alone with your stupid vegetarian food. I want a steak, or at least a burger. Fuck this whole eco shit!"

Taylor and Sean exchanged a meaningful glance. Sean rolled his eyes and Taylor raised her eyebrows.

"He should have known that this is a sustainable resort before he came," she said to Sean.

"With a little help from the bioengineering department," Sean scoffed. "The corals are artificial, not restored."

They heard the calming voices of waiters and hastily assembled management staff at the table behind them.

"I don't want to calm down," the loud and lubricated voice of the angry customer interrupted the soothing murmurs. "I am here on vacation. I pay good money. I don't want to be lectured on the environment and I certainly don't want to be told what I can or cannot do like a stupid schoolboy."

The sound of broken glass was followed by a crash and angry footsteps, as the furious guest stomped past them down the stairs to the beach.

Taylor and Sean got a blurry look at him in the moonlight and fire shine. The man was in his mid-fifties, overweight, with a beer belly, sunburnt, and with thinning hair, dressed in a cheap polyester Hawaiian shirt and sagging pants.

"Typical," Taylor said.

"Typical what?" Sean asked.

"You know, typical bitter white male in midlife crisis, disappointed with his life, blames others for his lack of success and happiness."

"You never know what goes on inside people." Sean smiled enigmatically.

"You can get a pretty good idea," Taylor insisted.

An anxious young server, wearing a natural cotton uniform from a local plantation, hurried after the angry customer.

"You can't take glass down to the beach, sir," she pleaded.

"Fuck your glass and fuck your beach, you stupid cow," the man yelled, and he threw the beer bottle in his hand in a high arc into the surf. The bottle spun around itself, eerily reflecting the moonlight, and in a perfect hyperbole, like a space capsule, it flew through the air and landed in the waves with a splash. The hotel employees gasped, and the young waitress covered her mouth with her hands.

"The alcohol, the glass, the reef . . ." she mumbled.

~

After a quick cup of Kona coffee and fresh, local fruit the next morning, Sean and Taylor ran down to the beach with their snorkeling gear. Taylor spit into her pink diving mask to prevent fogging, adjusted the snorkel in her mouth, and dove in. Just a few meters from the shore, an underwater canyon opened up and the magnificence of the reef unfolded in the filtered sunlight.

Taylor gasped and almost swallowed water at the sight of the colors and variety of corals and fish before her. What a difference from two years ago, when the reef had been blanched and dead. Now the reef revealed itself in a mind-blowing display of colors, shapes, and marine life. The corals had been genetically altered to withstand higher water temperatures brought on by global warming, but they were still sensitive to chemical substances. As part of their makeover, their shapes and colors had not just been restored but enhanced.

A dolphin made an impressive appearance right next to Taylor, emerging from behind a column of yellow, purple, and red brain coral into the sun rays filtering through from the surface. An entourage of small yellow surgeonfish followed behind and below, weaving through the underwater arches in psychedelic colors produced by the enhanced coral recreation. Taylor floated past fantastic columns and towers too elaborate to be created by nature. The dolphin swam right next to her in the shifting sunlight.

"Thank you," she signaled, "for admitting me into your realm."

The dolphin made a smooth turn as if in acknowledgment and dove down into an underwater canyon along jagged white and dainty pink finger corals. His entourage of blue surgeonfish surrounded him. He stopped in the middle of the canyon and looked back at her, as if to ask, "Are you coming?"

They both swayed with the waves, back and forth, up and down, but stayed pretty much in place. "Yes, I am here," she indicated with a nod. He turned with an elegant swish of his tail fin and dove deeper into the reef. She followed. They reached an underwater crevice with a sandy bottom, surrounded by a ring of sculpted rock. He stood still again, suspended between sandy ground and surface. He turned slightly so the sunlight struck his shiny back to full advantage, shimmering like liquid silver. The dolphin swayed a little longer with a school of yellow and black butterfly fish around him in a silent dance. He swam ahead of her and she realized he wanted to show her something. He turned back a few times to make sure she was still following. Taylor swam with the flow of the tide, riding the waves like the swarm of blue tang below.

They arrived at another underwater canyon, where three giant sea turtles swam around an imposing purple brain coral. The dolphin stopped and looked at her as if waiting for approval. She nodded, looking down past his shimmering body, and caught sight of something stuck underneath a rock on the bottom of the canyon. It didn't look right. It didn't belong here; the colors and the shape were all wrong—neon orange polyester fabric, and a thick, red piece of flesh sticking out on the other side of the rock.

Taylor gasped and swallowed salt water. She stuck her head above the surface and spit out water, gulping for breath. A body was wedged underneath a rock in the canyon, and she had a pretty good idea whose body it was.

~

Detective Tom Burke approached the terrace of the Coral Gardens Resort, glad to be wearing his blue Hawaiian shirt instead of a uniform. All the guests were in casual resort wear, and he wanted to blend in and not add more anxiety to the assembled group. Nobody was allowed to leave. So they sat at the wrought-iron tables, sipping their Kona coffee tensely.

The resort management had assigned him one of their offices for the interviews. His first guest introduced herself as Taylor Snider.

"Ms. Snider, can you tell me how you found the body?"

"I went out snorkeling early. A short time into my swim, a dolphin joined me. He swam alongside me and seemed eager to make contact."

"How did the dolphin try to make contact?" Burke asked skeptically.

"He turned his head and looked at me, to make sure I was following. I looked into his eyes. He appeared so friendly and intelligent."

"You know that the dolphins here have been trained as guardians of the reef, don't you?"

"I did not know that. What does that mean?"

"It means that a fleet of dolphins have been equipped with sensors and trained to detect behavior harmful to the reef, such as wearing sunscreen, throwing trash, or stepping on the fragile coral branches. As guardians of the reef, they watch and gently guide divers who do not conform back to shore."

"Well, I didn't have any chemical substances on me. I didn't wear sunscreen or deodorant. I was warned not to wear any. This dolphin clearly wanted me to follow him."

"How do you know it was male?" Burke sounded slightly annoyed.

"I don't. I just assumed. In any case, he or she swam ahead a little, then turned around to make sure I was coming until we reached the underwater canyon with the body. The dolphin wanted to show it to me, I am certain."

Burke raised his eyebrows, apparently not so certain about Taylor's interpretation of the dolphin's behavior. "Then what did you do?" he asked.

"I gasped, swallowed salt water, stuck my head above the surface, and took off my snorkel and mask. I tried to call for help, because I had no idea how to mark the spot with the body. I didn't think I could find it again without the dolphin's help."

"Did anybody notice you?"

"Yes, several swimmers closer to the shore saw me and alerted the lifeguards. They came out to me with their Jet Ski, and you know the rest."

Burke made a note on his papers before he continued. "Did you also witness the incident with one of the guests at dinner last night?"

"It's him, isn't it? He's the body? I only saw his leg under the rock, very red and bloated."

"I can't confirm that right now. But if you witnessed the incident last night, can you tell me about it in your own words?"

"One guest made a big scene about the vegetarian food and the eco-friendly rules. He yelled, broke a beer bottle, and called one staff person a stupid cow."

"Can you describe the guest in question?"

"Mid-fifties, overweight, angry, white, receding hairline, probably high blood pressure, because he was very red in the face. Does that fit the description of the body?"

"Sorry, I can't tell you."

"Oh, he was also very sunburnt. But he should have known before he came here that this is an eco-friendly resort."

"Probably, but Coral Gardens was acquired by EcoGuard Corporation only recently. Before that, the resort was in private ownership."

"I know, because we were here two years ago, and it was terrible."

Burke perked up. "How so? Why was it terrible?"

"It was called Black Rock Inn; it was run down and not very clean. The coral were bleached to a deadly white, and the owner was a grumpy alcoholic, always hunched over his computer. We left early and complained. When the renovated resort opened, the new owners contacted us and offered us a discount to come back. So here we are. Everything looks so much better. We love it. Until this incident, of course."

"Thanks, you've been very helpful. I will have to talk to you again. Unfortunately, none of the guests can leave the premises for now."

"But it was an accident, wasn't it?" Taylor asked. They were on vacation. This was paradise. No way a murder could happen on their first day here.

"At this point we are treating it as a suspicious death."

~

Flickering sunlight filtered through the coconut palms swaying in the trade winds in front of Tom Burke's interview room at the Coral Gardens Resort. He kept the windows open to feel the gentle breeze of salty air and hear the sound of the surf. The pleasant surroundings stood in stark contrast to the bundle of misery on the chair in front of him. He hated it when women cried. Instead of feeling protective, he was annoyed by the exaggerated display of emotion.

"Please compose yourself," he said to the young resort employee, whose name tag identified her as Imelda. She answered with a sob and blew her nose.

"Let's go over the events of last night again. Mr. Miller became very angry. Why was that?"

"He refused his dinner because it did not include any meat, and he didn't want to drink the organic wine. He wanted a burger, which we don't have on our menu. I brought him a bottle of beer and he called me a stupid cow." Imelda interrupted her narration with a sniffle. "Then he stormed off to the beach. I told him he couldn't take glass to the beach. The alcohol and glass are dangerous for the guests, the corals, and for the marine life, but he smashed the bottle and cursed at me." She blushed.

"Yes, we heard about that from the other guests. What did you do after that encounter?"

"I was very upset and ran into the kitchen to calm down and talk to my friend Maria. Maria and I came here together from the Philippines."

"How long were you in the kitchen?"

"Until about nine o'clock. Then I went to bed. They let me go early, because I wasn't much good for work anymore."

"So Maria, the other kitchen employee, can confirm this?"

"Yes." Imelda nodded vigorously.

"What did you do after nine?"

"I went to bed."

"Can anybody confirm that?"

"Am I a suspect? Do you really think I did anything to that man?"

"Please just answer the question. We are asking everybody where they were last night."

"I was in my bed, crying. I was afraid they might fire me. My daughter and mother at home depend on the money I send. I share a room with Maria, but she came in much later. She had to help clean up in the kitchen and restaurant." She was crying again.

Burke looked thoughtfully at the tiny woman in front of him. She barely weighed more than a child. Could she have dispatched a big, heavy man like Miller?

~

At eleven thirty, Burke and his colleague Detective Shepherd convened at the office with a cup of Kona coffee to compare notes.

"The coroner's report came in. Miller drowned, but it doesn't look like an accident. First of all, he had severe bruises all over his torso and on his temple. It's hard to determine what caused the bruises. It must have been a hard, but not very sharp, object," Shepherd reported.

"Could he have hit rocks after falling into the water?" Burke asked.

"It's a possibility, but the bruises are not consistent with hitting rocks. They are localized, induced by a blunt object."

"Unless the rocks were smooth and rounded?"

"They aren't at this part of the beach."

"Okay, what's the second point?" Burke said.

"The victim's body was wedged underneath a crevice, quite far away from shore. He was found in a fairly deep underwater canyon. He could not have drifted there after falling into the water, and he could not have dove down that deep by himself. Somebody wedged his body there beneath the rock; otherwise he would have washed up on the beach. Without the dolphin, it probably would have taken a long time to find him," Shepherd concluded.

"So, somebody murdered him and we have a resort full of suspects," Burke sighed. "What do we know about the victim?"

"Fifty-five years old, divorced, lived in Detroit. His construction business went bankrupt after a lawsuit convicted him of using defective, cheap pipes that contaminated the water supply with lead."

"What was he doing here?"

"It seems like he was here on the same deal as many of the other guests. EcoGuard Corporation offered them a promotion to their newly renovated resort because they had been to the hotel before, when it still was the Black Rock Inn and belonged to a private owner, who went bankrupt. EcoGuard took over for a song and a dance. They did a good job restoring it." Shepherd nodded toward the pristine beach and the native plant garden outside the window.

"Apparently it was not to everybody's taste."

～

Taylor and Sean sat in deck chairs facing the ocean.

"Do you want to go snorkeling?" Sean asked.

"Later. I am still a bit in shock," Taylor said.

"Finding a dead body will do that to you."

"I have a hard time believing something like murder could happen in paradise."

"Paradise may not be quite as idyllic as it looks," Sean considered.

"What do you mean?"

"Bioengineered corals, sensor-equipped dolphins as guardians . . ."

"It's the only way to save the coral," Taylor protested.

"When you mess with nature, there are always unforeseen consequences."

"Oh Sean, you are such a pessimist. I'm getting a massage."

"I'll stay here and wait for you."

~

The resort guests had assembled for sunset cocktails on the terraces. They radiated restlessness and tension. Nobody was allowed to leave the grounds. Taylor and Sean sipped their drinks silently. Resort staff supplied alcohol generously to calm their nerves. Shepherd and another police officer, both in Hawaiian shirts, sat at both ends of the terrace trying to look relaxed and inconspicuous. An agitated voice rose above the nervous chatter.

"Where is my wife? She went swimming hours ago and still hasn't come back. It's almost dark. What have you done to her? Did you kill her like that poor man yesterday?"

The police officers looked at each other and after a curt nod, Shepherd got up and approached the distraught guest, who was by now surrounded by staff trying to calm him down.

"Sir, please come with me," Shepherd said to the worried husband. He looked to be in his sixties, with a full head of white hair and skinny wrinkled legs that stuck out of his Bermuda shorts like toothpicks.

"Have you seen her?" he called to the assembled guests before the police led him away. "Blond, shoulder-length hair, pleasantly plump . . ."

With a firm hand, the police and staff led him inside. The decibel level of nervous chatter rose one notch. Several guests jumped up from their seats, and at least one cocktail glass fell over and spilled onto the volcanic pavers.

"Let's go for a walk along the beach," Taylor suggested. "It's getting a bit too intense for me here."

As they descended the stairs toward the beach, the police guard warned them, "Don't go beyond the resort boundaries and return by nightfall."

They nodded and continued.

"A lot of good that will do. Both disappearances happened within the resort boundaries and during daylight," Taylor observed.

"Mr. Miller disappeared after dark," Sean reminded her.

"True, there is a murderer out there in the darkness . . ." she said in a scary voice.

"Did you see the 'pleasantly plump' woman?" Sean asked.

"I think so. She sat next to me in a deck chair after you went back to the bungalow to work. We made some small talk. She and her husband are here from Mobile, Alabama. She works for an oil company. They just had an offshore oil spill and came here to recuperate from the stress of dealing with the aftermath of the lawsuits . . ." Taylor remembered.

"I wonder if any of the victims of the oil spill were able to recover from their damages with a Hawaiian vacation as well. I'm sure the pelicans weren't able to fly here with their oil-clogged feathers."

"I know, it's a tragedy. How much more human trash can this ocean absorb?"

They paused to look at the gentle waves, dipped in liquid gold by the setting sun. The foam of the breaking surf sent sparkling droplets into the cooling air. Waves broke and receded like a big, breathing organism.

"From here, it still looks very much alive," Taylor observed.

"Thanks to EcoGuard Corp," Sean said. "Looks can be deceiving."

"Maybe bioengineering is the only way to save the ocean."

"Hmm," Sean said as a dark object washed onto the beach with one of the powerful waves. The undertow pulled it back into the water, only to spit it out again with the next set of waves. They couldn't identify the object in the darkening red light.

"A surfer at this hour?" Taylor asked.

"This is no surfer." Sean accelerated his steps to approach the lifeless object.

"A dead fish?" Taylor called out hopefully, hurrying after him.

Sean had reached the surf. Lying facedown on the beach, all they could see of the object in the deepening darkness was a plump woman's body with matted blond hair in a messy ponytail.

~

At breakfast the next morning, Taylor and Sean sat pale and tired over their cups of Kona coffee with steamed milk. They glanced at the gray sea under an overcast sky. It reflected how they felt. They had barely slept; first because of all the interrogations they'd had to endure, second because they were in shock about finding another body, and third because the police and resort staff had begun treating them like suspects.

"What a vacation," Taylor sighed. "I wish I could go back to my desk at work and mind my own business."

"Look." Sean nodded toward the walkway leading to the resort lobby.

An attractive black woman in a tailored business suit and high heels pulled a carry-on over the pavers. The wheels of the suitcase clicked and clacked loudly on the uneven surface. All the guests stopped their conversations to watch.

"Who is she? The FBI?" Taylor wondered.

"I think they sent in the corporate investigator," Sean observed.

"What do you mean?"

"These deaths are very bad for EcoGuard's business."

"Obviously."

"I wonder how much has leaked out to the press and social media."

"I'm sure guests have posted the news on their Facebook and Instagram pages."

"Exactly. Who'd come here after two murders?" Sean said.

"How do you know the second death was a murder?" Taylor asked.

"Major bruises—I read about it online."

Taylor rolled her eyes.

~

The pleasant staff manager's office didn't look so pleasant anymore. Detective Tom Burke had spread files and reports everywhere. Notes were tacked on the walls. Dirty coffee cups and overflowing ashtrays covered all horizontal surfaces.

"Where is the maid service? It looks like a pigsty here," observed Karin Pinter as she entered, immaculately dressed in a white blouse, blue tailored jacket, and pencil skirt.

"I should ask you that question," Burke replied. "You work for EcoGuard." He squinted his bloodshot eyes and extinguished another cigarette in a saucer.

"You're not used to murders around here, are you?" Pinter remarked coolly as she cleared off several files and cups from a chair and sat down.

"We had five last year. How about you?" Burke shot back.

"We need to work together and compare notes if we want to solve this," Pinter said.

"Why should I share information with you?" Burke was in a foul mood.

"Damage control."

"That's your problem, not mine." Burke crossed his arms in a defensive gesture.

"Loss prevention, then."

"Loss of profit or loss of life?"

"Both," Pinter said calmly and crossed her shapely legs.

"What's your title, anyway?" Burke asked irritably. Pinter handed him her card. "Corporate Lawyer and Investigator for EcoGuard," he read out loud. "I'm sure the lawsuits are coming in hot and heavy." He placed the card on the desk in front of him.

"These incidents are ruining our reputation and costing us thousands of dollars every day. We need to stop them."

"Do whatever you need to do, but I have to solve two murders."

"So you have confirmed the second death was a murder," Pinter stated with satisfaction.

"Look. I can't involve you in the investigation, because the resort and some of its employees may be implicated. You know how it works," Burke said wearily. He hated women who tried to push him around and thought they always knew best.

"Exactly. That's why you need me. I can help you from the inside. It is in both of our interests to solve these deaths as soon as possible and find out who's responsible. You wouldn't want me to stonewall you, would you?"

Their eyes met and locked in a cold staring contest.

She is ice cold, he thought.

"You are not as foolish as you appear," she said, and broke the standoff with a smile.

He raised his eyebrows and shrugged. *Bossy black woman*, he thought.

"So how do we know that the second death, of"—Pinter looked at her notes—"Mrs. Mabel Corbin from Mobile, Alabama, was a homicide and not just an accidental drowning?"

Burke sighed. "This information is in the Coroner's report, so I am not giving anything away, but Mrs. Corbin shows the same bruising on the torso, neck, and temples as Mr. Miller. The bruises seem to have been inflicted with a blunt instrument or weapon. The victims' skin was not broken, which excludes sharp objects like knives."

"Could such a blunt object inflict enough damage to kill a person?" Pinter asked after taking careful notes.

"If it is directed with enough force to a person's temple or solar plexus, it can render the victims unconscious or even kill them."

"So you assume the cases are connected?"

"The method is consistent."

"Then why was the second body washed ashore, while the first one was wedged underneath a rock in an underwater canyon?"

"We're not sure. We're looking at people who had access to diving equipment and know how to use it. The location and depth of the first body was only accessible to a scuba diver."

"That probably includes everybody at this resort. According to my records there are twelve guests registered here. Well, given current events, we are down to ten," Pinter concluded matter-of-factly.

"Why so few?" Burke asked.

"The resort just reopened after extensive remodeling. This is our first batch of guests."

"You probably also know from your records that only four people took diving classes and used the equipment."

"That doesn't mean others don't know how to use it. We have the instructors and staff to consider."

"True," Burke considered. "We also have Taylor and Sean Snider from the Bay Area. They found both bodies, which seems a bit of a coincidence."

"Let's talk to them first," Pinter suggested.

"'Let's,' like in both of us?" Burke asked with irritation.

"I'll just sit in and share my observations. I'll have to talk to them anyway."

~

By the time Sean Snider sat down in the wicker chair with the floral-patterned natural cotton cushions, the interview room had been cleaned and organized. Behind the desk sat a disheveled Detective Burke and an impeccable Ms. Pinter, whose stern business suit looked completely out of place within the tropical décor.

"Mr. Snider, tell us about finding the two bodies," Detective Burke began.

"I only found the second body, or better, my wife Taylor and I almost stumbled over her on our walk last night. The first body was found by a dolphin, who then showed it to my wife."

"Yes, the dolphin," Burke said distractedly.

"What business are you in, Mr. Snider?" Karen Pinter interjected.

"I work for PharmaVision."

"They make optical sensors, don't they?" Pinter followed up. Burke shot an annoyed look at her.

"Among other things."

"What is the purpose of these sensors?"

"They have pharmaceutical applications such as detecting abnormal skin colorations, signaling potential high blood pressure or skin secretions containing toxins," Sean Snider explained. "How is this relevant?"

"Yes, how is this relevant, Ms. Pinter?" Burke echoed.

Pinter ignored them. "So you are aware of and familiar with the sensor technology our dolphins are equipped with?" she asked.

"It's based on one of our products. We never anticipated it would be used on animals, though . . ."

"Dolphins are very special animals. So potentially you have access to the visual stream coming in through the dolphin's sensors, which could contain images of the killer," Pinter stated with a triumphant look in Burke's direction.

"I'd say that is a pretty wild hypothesis," Snider challenged.

"It's a possibility we will follow up. Do you have access to this visual stream, Mr. Snider?"

"No, of course not. We sold EcoGuard the technology and software. It's a closed system. We don't access our clients' confidential stream."

"But if you really wanted, could you somehow gain access?"

"I don't think so. I don't even know how many dolphins have been equipped, and I also don't know where this questioning is going."

"A fleet of ten dolphins have been equipped with sensors and trained as guardians of the reef. Are you sure you didn't know that, Mr. Snider?" Pinter asked.

"No, I didn't, and I wasn't trying to find out. I am here on vacation, remember?"

"Thanks, Mr. Snider. That will be all." Pinter dismissed him.

Snider nodded and left. After he closed the door, Tom Burke exploded.

"You had no right to interrogate him like that and dismiss him. I had questions of my own I wanted to ask."

"Don't worry, we found out everything we need to know," Pinter said, and she lit one of Burke's cigarettes.

"I thought you weren't smoking," he protested.

"I am now," she replied and blew smoke at him.

"What did you find out from this interview that we needed to know? It was all about this unrelated sensor technology," asked Burke, coughing irritably.

"That he is lying." She stubbed out the cigarette.

"If you are smarter than Sherlock Holmes, then what was he lying about?" Tom Burke was losing his patience. This corporate lawyer was railroading his investigation.

"Mr. Snider knew very well how many dolphins had been equipped with sensors. He was one of the software engineers

EcoGuard worked with on this project," she said with cool, superior confidence.

"That's great, but he is still entitled to his vacation." Burke knew his rebuttal was lame. She had just delivered a valuable piece of information. Maybe it was worth the irritation to work in tandem with her. "Can you really recall the dolphin's visual feed?"

"It's not easy. I'm communicating with the technicians at headquarters about it."

"Where are your headquarters?"

"Palo Alto, California, Silicon Valley."

That explained her outfit, Burke thought. He had no sympathy for the snooty tech nerds in Silicon Valley. They were as far removed from the relaxed island vibe and the love for nature as he could imagine, even though they were just halfway across the Pacific Ocean. He had to admit, they also intimidated him, with their smart talk and their computer savvy. He still did things the old-fashioned way. "I guess we need to find out more about these sensors," he admitted. "They seem to be a key to this mystery."

"They've shown us a body; maybe they can show us the murderer too," Pinter said and yawned. *Ha, even she's not immune to jet lag*, Burke thought with satisfaction.

"Let's talk to the maid now." Pinter interrupted his thought stream.

"Imelda?"

"The one Mr. Miller called a 'stupid cow.'"

"Yes, ma'am," Burke sighed.

~

Imelda had been temporarily suspended from duty. When she came in, she wore a child-size pink hoodie with an appliquéd Winnie the Pooh. With one hand she clutched a soggy tissue, with the other the armrest of the wicker chair.

"I didn't do anything. How could I know he'd get so angry? I can't lose this job—my whole family in the Philippines depends on my paycheck," she sobbed.

Burke rolled his eyes, but Pinter picked up on something.

"Was the evening of his disappearance your first encounter with Mr. Miller?" she asked.

"No, I had been to his bungalow in the afternoon, when he ordered drinks and food from room service."

"What did he order?"

"He ordered steak, beer, and whiskey. We only have local goat stew on the menu as a meat dish, so I brought him that. He wasn't happy."

"What did he do?"

"First he yelled at me, and then he asked me to drink whiskey with him. I said no. I already knew he wasn't going to give me a tip," Imelda said.

"Did anything else happen?" Pinter asked.

Imelda let out a loud sob of despair. "He pulled me close to him and tried to kiss me. He was so disgusting, and smelled awful, of whiskey and smoke."

"You poor thing," Pinter said sympathetically and laid her hand on Imelda's arm. "So what did you do?"

"I tried to run away and twist out of his grasp, but he was so much bigger and heavier than me. He pinned me to the wall and put his tongue into my mouth and ear." Imelda was crying openly now.

"Why didn't you report him?" Burke asked, perplexed.

"He was a guest, a client—I couldn't cause a scandal. And who would have believed me? He put his hand down my shirt and cursed about all the buttons. I got so scared, I thought he was going to choke me or something else . . ." She blushed and her face twisted into a mask of fear, embarrassment, and disgust.

"I didn't think clearly. I just grabbed the fork from the tray I had brought and I rammed it into his thigh."

"Good girl," Pinter said, patting Imelda's hand.

"He screamed with rage, even though it couldn't have been that bad, but he let go of me for a second and I ran out."

"Well done, Imelda," Pinter said.

"No, not well done at all. If my manager finds out I stabbed a guest with a fork, he will fire me."

"Don't worry, he won't fire you. If this resort survives, I'll make sure you still have a job," Pinter said, trying to console her. "So when you saw Mr. Miller again that night, he was still furious with you."

Imelda nodded, her face streaked with tears. "He called me a stupid cow, and I was afraid he would tell my supervisor what I had done."

"Thank you, Imelda. You have been very brave and very helpful. You can go and get some rest now. Just don't leave the resort."

She looked at them with big eyes. "Where would I go?"

After she left the room, Burke said, "She has a motive."

"And how would a ninety-pound girl drown a two-hundred-fifty-pound man who was at least two heads taller than her?"

"With an accomplice—or luck."

~

Outside in the corridor, Taylor sat on a sofa, enjoying the cool draft from a ceiling fan spinning overhead and the breeze from the open French doors at the end of the hallway. Across from her sat one of the diving instructors, named Pete. They both watched Imelda emerge from the interview room, dissolved into tears. She ran past them.

"What did they do to her?" Taylor asked.

The diver just shrugged. "I guess everybody is a suspect," he said gruffly. He knew Tom Burke from town and drank beers with him on occasion, so he wasn't overly worried.

~

Pete Camry shifted uncomfortably around the easy chair in the manager's office. He was an outdoors type. In an office he was out of his element. Pinter observed him coolly and quietly for a minute or two. That made him squirm even more.

"Where were you two nights ago?" Burke finally asked.

Pete looked at him, almost grateful someone had broken the silence. Another guy.

"I was with my buddies. I don't live at the resort. I live in Lahaina. We went out to Fleetwood's. A couple of our friends played in the band there that night."

"So your friends could confirm your alibi?"

"Yes, I can give you their names. There were five of us." Pete sounded smug.

Burke nodded, satisfied.

"What time did you get to the bar?" Pinter asked.

"It must've been around ten. The set didn't start until then."

Pinter looked at Burke sharply with a raised eyebrow.

"Where were you before ten?" she wanted to know.

"I finished up here in the dive shack, made sure all the equipment was stored and in order. Then I had a bite to eat."

"Where did you eat?"

"Just at the Fast Food."

"Do you have any witnesses for the time before ten o'clock?"

Pete looked at her, surprised. "No, I don't. Am I a suspect?"

Burke came to his aid. "Was all the diving equipment in order and accounted for?"

"As far as I remember. I made sure it was all organized and clean of salt water, because that erodes the rubber seal of the mask." Pinter nodded impatiently.

"Did you take stock of the number of diving masks, snorkels, and oxygen tanks?" Burke asked, offering him a safety ring. Pete finally got it.

"I may not have counted exactly how many pieces of diving equipment were present at the time," he admitted.

"So someone could have taken a set and gone out on the reef?" Burke said.

"That's possible."

"How is the diving equipment secured when it's not in use?" Pinter asked.

"It's pretty secure—we have a padlock with a pass code," Pete said proudly. Burke rolled his eyes.

"Who has the access code?" Pinter got up and stood in front of Pete, looking down at him. Predictably, he squirmed again. He also had a sheen of sweat on his face. Not one to hold up well under pressure.

"It's on a sticky note on the break room refrigerator."

"Pete, that means anybody could have gotten it. I didn't know you ran things so sloppily around here," Burke exclaimed.

"Thanks, Mr. Camry—we have no other questions," Pinter said.

Pete ambled out of the room as fast as he could.

"That wasn't much help," Pinter summed up. "He doesn't have an alibi, and anybody on staff could have accessed the dive shack and taken out equipment that night."

"That pretty much sums it up," Burke confirmed.

~

Nobody went into the water that day. The guests lay on deck chairs under natural cotton umbrellas and watched the dolphins frolic around the reef. They even showed off some impressive jumps to the captive audience, twisting their glistening bodies in the sunlight like quicksilver.

Karen Pinter sat on the armrest of the easy chair in her resort room overlooking the beach. She had kicked off her high heels and held a cell phone to her ear.

"Lars, we need to go through the visual feed from the dolphin fleet at Coral Gardens Maui right away. I know there are ten dolphins, but this is a top priority. The dolphins must have seen the killer. Put some people on it. Lives may depend on it, not to mention our reputation and profit. We can probably identify him through their feed."

"There is just a little problem with that, Karen," said a male voice through the speaker phone.

"What's the problem? Can't you see how important this is?"

"I realize that, but we have a little technical problem."

"What do you mean?" She got up and paced the room irritably.

"I mean we don't have access to the dolphins right now."

"What's wrong?"

"A little glitch probably, a malfunction. I'm sure we can fix it."

"Since when?" Pinter asked sharply.

"Two days, give or take. We weren't exactly monitoring all our dolphins around the world twenty-four/seven," Lars said wearily.

"You lost touch with all the dolphins at all our resorts around the world?"

"We're on it, Karen—we didn't see the urgency."

"Lars, we have two murder victims here. If we don't solve and stop this right now, we may both be out of a job."

"We are doing our best. But I suspect there may be a hostile intruder in the system."

"What does that mean?

"A hacker, most likely."

"Jeez, Lars, why would anybody hack into our dolphin data?"

"You tell me, Karen. I am clueless here."

"This is really bad. Try to fix it asap."

"Will let you know."

Pinter hung up. She looked out onto the beach where the guests sat huddled and miserable in their deck chairs, staring at the ocean. What a disaster! EcoGuard had invested millions in this resort, including the coral-saving technology, and now, only a few weeks after the opening, it looked doomed. News about the *"Deaths in Paradise,"* as the *Honolulu Star-Advertiser* dubbed them, had spread all over the media. Who would come here now?

She noticed the cute brunette with the ponytail, Sean Snider's wife, getting up and gathering her diving gear. She approached the water together with one of the dive instructors, Pete, who didn't have an alibi. They put on their diving gear and prepared to enter the water. Sean Snider looked on from his deck chair.

"No!" Pinter screamed and ran outside. She was barefoot, but her pencil skirt limited her stride. "No!" she screamed again as she pulled up her skirt. "Don't go into the water!" She stumbled and stubbed her toe on a rock as she rushed to the shore. Pete didn't react to her screams, either because he didn't hear or because he didn't want to. He was on their suspect list. "Stop!" she yelled, and finally Taylor turned her head in Pinter's direction. Gasping and out of breath, Pinter reached the beach.

"Don't go into the water," she panted.

Taylor looked at her. "Why not?" she asked. "We can't just sit around all day. We are on vacation. We paid for this," she complained.

"I'm sorry, Mrs. Snider, but we cannot guarantee your safety in the water right now." Pinter looked at the dive instructor, who shrugged and began taking off his gear. "Thank you—we don't want to take any chances."

Taylor walked back to her deck chair, pouting.

"Mr. Snider, could I have a word in my office, please?" Pinter asked, and then directed the other guests on the beach. "Please don't go into the water today. We hope to solve these incidents within a day or two, and then you can leave or continue your vacation as planned."

Her announcement was greeted with annoyed mumbling. Sean Snider closed his laptop and carried it under his arm, ready to accompany Karen Pinter.

~

"Mr. Snider, what is your position within PharmaVision?" Pinter asked.

"I'm a software engineer."

"We need your help. Can you get access to the dolphins' visual data from their sensors?"

"It would be unethical and technically illegal for me to access that visual stream. You should ask your technicians at EcoGuard," Sean protested.

"I did, but they have a problem. A computer glitch. They can't access the stream."

"They can trouble-shoot with our tech support. I'm sure they can work it out."

"It may not be that easy. It looks like someone deliberately disabled our access."

"Then they should follow the digital trail and find out who did it."

"I want you to do it."

"Me? You want me to hack into your system? I can lose my job for that and I can be prosecuted."

Pinter pulled out several papers from a folder and put them on a desk in front of Snider.

"We have prepared a legal document here, stating that you are helping in a murder investigation. It's signed by Detective Burke, from the Maui Police Department, and me, corporate lawyer and investigator of EcoGuard. It frees you from all liability." Pinter stood up straight and pulled down her skirt, which was still hiked above her knees from her run to the beach. She tried hard to look like a respectable lawyer. Detective Burke nodded gravely.

"Jeez, you guys must be desperate." Sean Snider looked at the documents.

"We are. And time is of the essence. You know the software, you know the system, you can get access and follow the trail of whoever disabled it."

"You have a lot of confidence in me. I'm not sure I can do this, but I'll give it a shot. Just wondering, how do you know you can trust me? I could be the one who disabled the system."

Pinter smiled. "I don't think so. You were completely uncon-cerned when your wife tried to go scuba diving earlier today. If you knew about a concrete danger, you wouldn't have let her go so easily."

Snider ginned. "I like your conclusions. Okay, I'll do my best. Give me a few hours." He grabbed his laptop and left.

~

When he was gone, Tom Burke opened a folder.

"We received the complete autopsy report. Most of it we know. The interesting part is the murder weapon. It's difficult to define and even harder to identify. A hard, blunt object, applied with great force, as if the attacker had taken a run and then rammed the weapon into the victims. It is hard, but not hard enough to break the skin; I have no idea what it could be. A coconut? Or a baseball bat?"

Pinter looked past him, out the window at the beach, where at this moment two dolphins jumped into the air, followed a glittering arch, and reentered the water gracefully.

"A dolphin's snout," she exclaimed excitedly. "A dolphin, or several, rammed the victims with their snouts. It makes sense; they are the guardians of the reef, and the victims were environmental offenders. Mr. Miller contaminated the water supply, and Mabel Corbin was implicated in an oil spill."

"No way. The dolphins would never harm a human being. They are not capable by nature or by training. Plus, how would they know about the victim's environmental crimes?" Burke protested.

"If someone hacked into their system, they could have changed the criteria of who constitutes a risk to the reef and how to deal with them," Pinter offered.

"Who could have done anything like that?" They looked at each other.

"Sean Snider."

They got up and ran out the door.

~

Sean Snider looked up in surprise as Karen Pinter and Tom Burke burst into his bungalow.

"Take your hands off that computer," Burke demanded. "Put them in the air where we can see them." Burke had drawn his weapon, which seemed a bit unnecessary now. So he waved it at Snider and then put it back into his waistband.

Slowly, Snider lifted his hands off the keyboard and held them up high.

"Mr. Snider, you are under arrest for the murder of Mr. Miller and Mabel Corbin using dolphins as weapons," Burke declared.

"You are the only one who had the access, knowledge, and skills to manipulate the data," Pinter followed up.

Snider looked at them completely expressionless.

"Are you done?" he asked. "I found the computer breach," he said calmly, "and I followed its trail back to this island."

"Maui," Burke stated unnecessarily. He was ready to arrest this man, but now . . .

"If you have a boat, I think we can locate the computer from which the hack originated. It's right here on the Kaanapali coast."

"Inside the resort?" Pinter asked.

"No."

Burke and Pinter looked at each other, weighing their options. To trust or not to trust? Was he a murderer or the solution? Snider already had his laptop under his arm and was moving rapidly toward the small pier on the beach, where a midsize leisure boat was docked for guests. Burke and Pinter followed. Pinter waved for assistance and hiked up her skirt to climb on board. A staff member ran down from the main building to navigate the boat for them.

"Where are you going, Sean?" Taylor called from the beach, waving at them to wait for her. "Can I come?"

"I'll be right back—don't worry," Sean called back, as the boat started and launched.

It tuckered along Maui's verdant coastline, going north past Napili toward the rugged Kapalua coast.

"We're getting close," Snider said, scanning his computer for the location signal.

"Should we worry?" Pinter asked.

A gunshot rang out. It came from a dense palm grove at the shore. Burke returned fire.

"Shit." Pinter ducked behind the side of the boat, and Sean tried to shield his computer.

Another round of shots—and then quiet. Very quiet. Only the tuck-tuck of the boat engine and the lapping of the water against the hull could be heard. Burke stared at the shore, weapon drawn.

"Damn, I lost the signal," Snider said.

"Is it moving? Is he retreating?" Pinter asked anxiously.

"No, he just turned off the computer, or disconnected it."

"We have to go ashore. I'm calling for backup," Burke announced.

"We are very exposed here," Pinter considered.

"I think he left," Snider speculated.

"I am going in. Take us closer," Burke demanded. A nervous boat operator navigated the craft closer to the coast until Burke could jump out and wade ashore, weapon drawn. Several tense minutes passed.

"It's all clear here. You can come in," they heard him call from the palm grove. Snider and Pinter, who had by now torn a long slit in her skirt, jumped overboard and walked up the beach into the grove.

A hammock hung between two palms and a small hut nestled between the trees. A wooden table with a chair and a laptop stood close to the beach, but hidden by the grove. Radio antennas were wired up to palm trees.

"That's the computer." Snider sat down and opened the laptop.

"Be careful," Pinter warned, but Snider had already booted up, and a message appeared on the screen.

"Congratulations, you found me—or at least my computer. You have ruined paradise, you have ruined my life, and the lives of the dolphins. You have taken away my Black Rock Inn and replaced it with your sterile Coral Gardens. Well, enjoy! Good luck guessing what the dolphins are going to do next." A picture of a dolphin with red eyes appeared before the screen went black and, with a hissing sound, short-circuited the system.

6

DREAM DRIVER - LADAN MURPHY

The alarm woke Marjorie up at 5:30 a.m. from a nightmarish sleep about roads, cars, and crashes. She prepared and headed out to the television station for her interview with World Market News (WMN) about the advancement of her company, where she'd worked for the last eight years.

∼

"*Dream Driver Corp* has been in the news lately. This afternoon, we have Marjorie Morrison, Vice President of Data and Security, here to get some answers," the reporter announced on air.

Marjorie's dark hair was neatly pulled back in a bun, her makeup tastefully in place, and her tailored navy pantsuit snug on her body as she sat under the light next to the reporter.

The reporter turned to face her. "Marjorie, can you tell us a little about *Dream Driver*?"

"*Dream Driver* produces the Safe Guard Life System, which includes two modules. One drives the car automatically, and the other determines the best course of action and least cost to human lives in case of an accident. When combined, these two modules provide the safest and most effective means of trans-porting people," Marjorie said.

"What is *Dream Driver's* plan for integrating these modules in the automotive market space?" the reporter asked.

"As you know, the bill to mandate all cars to be self-driving by the year 2025 will be up for congressional approval and we are expecting it to pass easily. We are working closely with car manufacturers to put a Safe Guard Life System in every car. This will be a major breakthrough for our company while providing consumers a self-driving unit with lifesaving features."

"*Dream Driver* is facing some controversies for self-driving car crashes which have resulted in the deaths of several people. Do self-driving cars really save lives?"

The question, although expected, made her uncomfortable. "Of course. Have you seen the rate of fatalities in human-oper-ated car accidents? There are always glitches to be worked through. If we expected any technology to be perfect, we wouldn't be driving cars today," Marjorie said as she felt the heat rise in her face. She quickly regained her composure and continued: "Technology always moves forward, and we at *Dream Driver* are positioning ourselves at the top."

"How about the claim that your product is not ready for market yet? A young, promising engineer died in a self-driven car with a *Dream Driver* system just two weeks ago."

"Sometimes accidents are inevitable. You have to consider that without the lifesaving algorithm, multiple lives could have been lost in the accident."

"According to Alert News, the lifesaving algorithm list used in the Safe Guard Life System disproportionally saves the lives of the rich and politically connected. How do you answer these allegations?" the reporter asked.

"That is not true. The algorithm in the Data Point Module doesn't consider a person's income or political status; it simply decides based on the highest possible survival chance. We don't artificially change the outcome, and it is solely an algorithmic-based calculation."

"How about yet another accident in which a male passenger lost his life when the car crashed itself in order to avoid hitting a woman? Some say this is an example of negligence on your company's part."

Marjorie took a deep breath. "While the loss of the man's life is tragic, this doesn't indicate a flaw in the Safe Guard Life System; rather, the system performed as intended by avoiding the scenario, which had a 76.7 percent chance of killing both the young mother of two and the male driver. The algorithm is meant to find the best possible solution to save lives and it doesn't always work in everyone's favor, just most."

"That is all we have time for today. Please come back and let us know about *Dream Driver's* progress, and thank you for being with us today, Marjorie," the reporter said as he moved on to the next segment of the news.

~

"Well done, Marjorie!" Ron Williams, the chief technology officer of *Dream Driver Corp*, texted.

Back at the office Marjorie dreaded facing Lori, the Vice President of Technology. Lori's approval meant a lot. Lori had created the Deterministic Algorithm Module, or DAM, which enabled self-driving cars to evaluate the road conditions and sense object movements.

"Us girls should stick together," Lori used to say. Lori had hired Marjorie, she had cheered her every achievement, and she had championed her promotion to Vice President of Data and Security to become her own equal. But Lori had become sinister with Marjorie's work on the Data Point Module. Marjorie had signed off on the release of the DPM to include the override function on the Priority List. Lori argued that DPM was a technology open to manipulation and corruption. She had encouraged Marjorie to block human override and leave the module completely algorithm driven, solely based on human safety.

Lori was everything that Marjorie wanted to be. Lori hadn't

gone to a university as prestigious as Marjorie's, nor had she finished her PhD like Marjorie, but still their diplomas didn't measure them in the right order of their brilliance. Marjorie always studied long and worked hard for every achievement. She envied Lori's effortless accomplishments, her way of sprouting ideas and flawlessly implementing them.

Marjorie's heart was beating fast as she headed to Lori's office. She stopped to take a deep breath before entering. *I don't care if she doesn't approve of the override; that is what has put me over the top. I have earned this, the corner office, the position—I have earned it all. My hard work is finally paying off and I am not apologizing for it. God knows Lori always gets what she wants in her life,* she thought.

Lori, in her usual casual jeans and plain shirt, seemed in deep thought with her head leaned back on her armchair, her eyes staring at the ceiling. Her neck bent backwards, and her short blond hair touched her shoulders. Marjorie had always admired how comfortable Lori was in her own skin.

Lori lowered her head to see Marjorie at her office door.

"Come in." Lori turned her swivel chair to face Marjorie, who sat across from her. The cold look in her eyes made Marjorie regret coming into her office.

Marjorie couldn't help noticing a picture of Lori with her husband and her teenage daughter, their arms around each other, next to a Mother's Day card that read "You are the best mom ever" on Lori's desk. Marjorie envied Lori's closeness with her family. Marjorie and her husband kept a cordial relationship for their son's sake. She wished her son valued her technical achievement instead of his father's boat rental business.

Marjorie turned at the sound of a knock on Lori's door. "That was an excellent interview, Marjorie," Ron said. "Nice touch on mentioning the woman's two children for the downtown accident."

Lori went off: "Yes, nice job not talking about the override you designed in your Priority List Data Points, Marjorie.

Remember that woman, the drunken loser with a rich daddy whose life you saved, while sleeping at night?"

The grudge in Lori's voice stirred Marjorie's sense of defiance. Her teeth clenched, and her fists closed so tight that her nails dug into her palms.

"The chance of a drunkard with connections and money jumping in front of a car is almost statistically zero. So what if we saved one? You are the architect of the Deterministic Algorithm Lifesaving System; without it my Data Point System would be nothing. Maybe I should think of *you* when I sleep," Marjorie sneered.

"Do you even think about the statistically nonexistent father of the teenage son who spent twenty-two days in a coma before he died from the accident?" Marjorie felt the burn of the fury in Lori's eyes. "Did we even try to save his life and make it right by helping him with his costs?"

"He was a person of no significance. The math to save his life doesn't work out; the cost of saving his life outweighs his value to society," Ron said.

"It's good to know there is a dollar sign on the back of every person walking out there," Lori said with a smirk.

"There is a price for everything. This is an unfortunate fact of life," Ron said.

"How about that young engineer, Ron, what was the price for his life?" Lori asked.

"You are out of line, Lori. Thank God I can rely on you, Marjorie." Ron walked out the door, but not before Lori shouted, "Oh, getting testy! It takes two kills to get you angry; maybe you are developing a conscience after all."

"It's a done deal; I signed off on the release of the Data Point System, override and all," Marjorie said.

"Is there anything fair in your Data Point System, Marjorie?" Lori asked.

Blood rushed through Marjorie's head, and her vocal cords harshened.

"You hired me, you mentored me, you helped me all the way.

Just be happy for me. Why do you have to be so sarcastic all the time?" Marjorie stood up to leave Lori's office.

"I am leaving this company, Marjorie. I thought I could make a difference, but I was wrong. We're just their foot soldiers. That is all. They have bent what could be a great benefit to save lives to serve their purpose." Lori's voice softened slightly with her last words as Marjorie walked out of her office.

~

The next day, Ron called Marjorie to his office. As she approached, she heard him on the phone through the narrow crack of his tenth-floor office door.

"Sir, we have to deal with Lori. She is acting up, threatening to go to the media."

After a pause, Ron continued: "Yes, of course, I understand. I will take care of it."

The door creaked as Marjorie pushed it open, and Ron turned around to face her.

"Oh, Marjorie, come on in." Then, with a somber face, he continued: "I want to let you know Lori has been taken off the project."

"That is a bit drastic. I'm sure Lori will come to her senses," Marjorie said, hoping Lori wasn't serious about leaving the company.

"We'll see. It is a shame. With her brilliant mind, she could accomplish so much more," Ron said.

Lori will make up with Ron again. She wouldn't want to miss all the brilliant ideas she wanted to implement in the newer versions of their product, Marjorie thought.

"I have a gathering at my house on Memorial Day weekend. I'd like you to come and meet Senator Torrance. It's a good opportunity for you to show off your stellar work and for him to see the brilliant minds behind the Data Point Module," Ron said.

"Of course, I'll be there. Thank you," Marjorie responded.

∾

A week later, the news of Lori being critically injured in an accident went around the office. A sense of worry tumbled through Marjorie's stomach. She wondered if the accident was staged, if the Deterministic Algorithm and Priority List had been tampered with via a faulty sensor and an override on the Data Point System. She had a bad feeling about Ron's involvement in it. *What had he meant by Lori being out of line and he would take care of it? Did Lori get checkmated?*

Marjorie rushed to the hospital. Her heart dropped when she saw Lori's bruised face and bandaged head through the glass window of her hospital room. She was hooked up to a life-support machine. Lori's husband shouted, "Get the hell out of here! I don't want any of you people from *Dream Driver* near her. You all did this to her."

Marjorie remembered how much she had admired Lori. She had considered Lori a friend, a person she could rely on. She liked how Lori said "Mar" quickly and dragged "jorie" when she called her name. She liked when Lori threw her head back and laughed wholeheartedly. And mostly she liked how Lori was always available for everyone on her team.

At home, in the shower, under the running water, Marjorie hit the walls with her arms as tears ran down her face furiously. Out in the world she had to be tough and unshakable, but in the shower a small, soft part of her heart not yet hardened by her harsh world took over.

For now, Marjorie tried to put Lori out of her mind and to concentrate on how to present herself at Ron's gathering successfully. She wished she hadn't designed the Priority List override to unfairly give priority to people of influence and power in DPM. The monster she created had taken on a life of its own and she had no way of controlling it.

∾

The day of the party, Marjorie prepared herself with rehearsed lines for ideas and talking points before she drove in her preferred manual drive to the top of the hill to Ron's house. At the soiree, Marjorie focused on spotting Senator Torrance through the crowd of guests and waiters with trays of food and drinks. She found him inebriated beyond what she would expect of his status, talking incoherently and wobbling, about to fall over.

How hard I have worked to impress this man!

It was not long before she decided to leave. The hired valet brought her car. She was driving along the winding road down the hill when she noticed a car in the middle of the road speeding toward her. She drove a little farther, looking for a turnout to pull over and let the car pass, but the car automatically kicked into self-drive mode and moved toward the middle. She saw Senator Torrance in the mirror in the car behind her. Frantically, she struggled to take back control of the car. The deafening sound of metal crashing into her car came after a loud screech. She was thrown forward and hit the exploding air bag, and then she lost sight of the road. She could feel the sharp pain of her broken ribs. The MAS voice unit repeated: "Full break applied." But the inertial force pushed the car to the edge and then off the road. All went black after a sharp fall.

~

"She is paralyzed from the neck down. With extensive therapy, some of her nerve damage may be repaired over time, but there are no guarantees," the doctor said before walking out of the room.

Marjorie heard the conversations in her groggy state.

The phone rang. Ron's voice echoed in the white hospital room, talking on his cell phone.

"Just a tragic accident. The self-drive sensors overrode the system in both cars to slow down the senator's car. Marjorie's car took the impact. What are we going to do about her?" Ron said after a little pause, "I understand. I already have her replacement in place; he has half her talent and twice her ambition. On the upside, he will be loyal and will do what he is asked." The one-sided conversation continued. "Torrance will push the mandate of self-driving cars with lifesaving algorithm in the Senate this week."

Marjorie opened her eyes to see Ron walk toward her and stand over her bed in the hospital room.

"What a tragic accident. What are the chances of Torrance and you driving on the road at the same time? The DAM in the car sensed the imminent danger and overrode the drive. The DPM, your own module, then determined to save the senator; millions of dollars are invested in him, you understand, Marjorie? It is not personal; we'll do what we can for you, of course."

Marjorie felt a single tear running down the side of her face and the tube inside her right cheek. She hoped her son would never find out about her part in the Priority List.

She remembered *the man of no significance*. She was no different; she had known it since she saw Lori in the hospital. She wondered how long it would take Lori's husband to use the e-mail she sent him before heading to the party, an e-mail with the list of wealthy and influential people Ron had put on the over-ride list.

Lori would be proud of me now, Marjorie thought.

7

SAVING GRACE - LINA KAROLINE CASTILLO

Grace hesitated, then knocked softly on Branson's office door. The boss looked up from the layouts of the next issue of *Island Escapes* piled on his desk. The door was closed, but the editor-in-chief saw her through the slim, horizontal metal louvers that shuttered the windowed office walls. He'd adjusted the rust-colored mini-blinds so he saw not only who was waiting, but what was going on in the small but bustling newsroom beyond.

"Ah, our timid new graphic designer," Branson said to himself and smiled. Grace stood outside the door, head lowered, black librarian glasses draped over her mousy hair. "This should be fun."

"Enter."

"Good morning, Mr. Branson."

"Branson, just call me Branson." He chewed on the red grease pencil used to make changes to magazine layouts. An unlit Marlboro cigarette sat in a clean ashtray among the layouts, photos, caffeine-stained mug, and clutter on his desk.

"Well, Mr. Branson, I mean Branson, sir." Grace stepped a bit closer. "I was assigned the 'Living on Margarita Island' feature article, and I have a few ideas, but—"

"But what?" Branson cut her off and looked at the young woman in a disheveled sweater over baggy jeans, her eyes weary green, the color of the Puget Sound on a cloudy day.

"Well, the artwork's due on Friday. But the writer and photographer haven't turned their files over to me, and I, um, wasn't sure what—"

"That article is a major spread in our next issue," the editor interrupted. "Our readers fantasize about leaving their dismal, dreary lives behind, dropping everything except their sunglasses so they can go live on a tropical island we've told them—*showed* them—is paradise."

He had not yet dismissed her, but his attention returned to the layouts on his desk. "You know, this is your chance to prove yourself. I want to see something today."

Grace bit her lip. *How am I supposed to know what it is like to live on a tropical island when the closest I've gotten to a beach is West Seattle, where the typical beachwear is sweats?*

She couldn't hold back the sigh.

Branson looked up from the layout of "The Colorful Island of Burano" on his desk. Grace was still standing there. He thought back to last hunting season in the oak country above the east end of the Columbia River Gorge, and the look of surprise in the deer's eyes before he squeezed the trigger.

Grace had that same look. *Must be lonely, nearing thirty, single, no fun in her life.*

"Look, I know you're new and the office manager is out, but I'll make sure she gets on the writer's case. Meanwhile, here's my advice. Go back to your desk and pretend you are on that exotic Caribbean island, and imagine everything it offers. Give me something good. It's a four-page center spread, so 'Greek' it at twelve hundred words."

The doe-eyed woman blinked.

"You know, Lorem Ipsum, placeholder text?"

"Yes, of course, I know what Greeking, what Lorem Ipsum, is."

"Good. Shut the door on the way out."

Grace closed the door with moist palms and headed straight for the restroom. Her stomach wrenched. She threw up her tuna sandwich lunch in the toilet, cleaned up, and faced herself in the mirror. *You can do this. You have to do this.*

On the way back to her cubicle, Grace stopped at the photo desk. She googled "Margarita Island" to find out what she could on what the locals called "Isla de Margarita."

"Of course," she said to herself, learning that the island was where Jimmy Buffett wasted away. She downloaded Buffett's *Meet Me in Margaritaville: The Ultimate Collection* to her iPod and popped in her earbuds.

The next three hours drifted away as the tiny Caribbean island off the coast of Venezuela came to life.

Pleased with her opening page, Grace moved on to the center spread. She anchored it with a photo of a beach scene from Playa El Agua, the most popular beach on the island. A single palm tree leaned over gold sand toward the turquoise bay, its thin leaves dancing over the blue-green foam, colorful windsurfers catching the waves in the distance. Marshmallow clouds tried hard but didn't dull the sun's bright rays across the top of the page.

She filled the article with the placeholder text to substitute for the author's headlines, copy, and captions.

At three o'clock, Grace leaned back, arms overhead, and stretched. Pleased, she saved her file and left to get a cup of every Seattleite's favorite brew at the corner Starbucks.

Grace walked back to the concrete office tower in downtown Seattle with her triple mocha latte. Grateful for the drink that warmed her hands and heart, she raised the hood of her wool coat and daydreamed of living in a place where all you'd ever want to order is something cold to drink.

Back in the office, a rejuvenated Grace slipped off her gloves, scarf, and coat and returned to her computer. At a single click, the project opened on the wide computer screen.

But the file was different. The make-believe text had disappeared. In its place were real words. The headline now read: "Amazing Grace: Life on Margarita Island." Eyes wide, Grace read the first few lines of the article.

"Grace Schmidt, 29, found her life's work—and passion—on Margarita Island. She moved there on a whim, from Seattle, Washington, in February 2011 . . ."

"What the heck?" Grace said out loud, spilling some of the flavored coffee on her keyboard. Ignoring it, she read on. Every word, every caption, was about a woman, a woman with her name, her, living on Margarita Island.

Even the women in the photographs resembled her: the woman on the beach in her bikini; the one horseback riding; the one laughing with the locals, lingering at the colorful shops, sipping a drink on the beach in the company of a handsome man, biting into the flesh of a mango picked right off a tree.

Only that woman couldn't be her. That tanned, laughing woman had fun, a purpose in life, and looked happy, oh so happy.

"A laid-back life with a South American vibe" is how the article described it, "slow-paced, no matter how important the stuff you thought you had to do."

Grace leaned back in her chair and did an inventory of her life.

Derek came to mind.

Last Friday, she had come home from work with takeout Chinese to find him sitting on the sofa with a packed bag at his side, ready to bolt. "I'm sorry," he said, his right hand massaging his eyebrow. He always did that when he was upset.

"You have nothing more to say? After living with me for six months?" she asked, trying to control the shaking as she sunk into the opposite side of the couch where they ate pizza and beer, and binge-watched season one of *The Walking Dead*, all winter long.

Derek shrugged and said, "We tried, but it's not enough, Grace, not for either of us. I know you're not happy. It didn't work. We need to move on."

He put his keys to the apartment on the coffee table, came over and kissed her forehead, and left. She took the container of sweet-and-sour pork out of the brown bag, opened the lid, took a bite with the wooden chopsticks, and chewed.

Grace could have called a friend, but she had no one she wanted to call.

Not even her mom, who hadn't returned her texts or letters since moving to Montana with her newest husband 18 months ago. Or her older sister, Emily, who lived a perfect Percocet life with her professor husband and two perfect kids in Eugene. Grace had called and asked if she could visit and stay for a while last summer. "Not a good idea," was Emily's curt answer.

~

Grace blinked and looked around. Was she predetermined to work in a square concrete building, within a square cubicle where she looked out over the weary, fog-laden sound? Where she only dreamt of life lived in a faraway land, a land with always smiling sun-tanned people doing things they loved?

"Hah! I'm just like our readers." Grace laughed. "Branson would get a kick out of that."

She turned to the last page of her layout.

The photo she'd placed there had changed. Instead, there *she* was, in the Caribbean town. She was the smiling woman with orange-painted toenails in the flowing, white gauze dress, wearing a coconut-fiber hat with fresh flowers on its brim. She was the woman with intense green eyes that peered at a sign pasted on the window of the first floor of a parrot-blue building. The sign said "Wanted: Graphic Designer / Art Director for *El Sol de Margarita*, Daily Newspaper. Must have talent, imagination, and like to laugh."

Grace sucked in her breath and touched her fingers to the

screen to zoom in on the Wanted sign. She grabbed a pen and jotted down the phone number and e-mail address.

~

From inside his office, Branson's eyes caught the commotion.

He watched Grace turn off her computer, grab her purse, and get up to leave. He was about to go into the workroom and inquire about the article when Grace stopped. She sat, hands in her lap.

Branson sighed.

Grace bit her lip and opened the bottom right desk drawer. She leaned over and scrambled around in a rush, searching for something. It took a full minute before she found what she was looking for. She grabbed the sunglasses and nearly ran out of the building, leaving her gray wool coat on her chair.

Behind the rust-colored blinds, Branson smiled.

8

THE BANYAN TREE - LINA KAROLINE CASTILLO

Mitsumi Haramoto once loved the great big banyan tree. It stood in the center of 'Aiea, a small sugarcane town west of bustling Honolulu. The tree was downhill from the sugar mill, the lifeblood of the town, where 'Aiea Heights Drive met Moanalua Road.

The banyan was only eight feet tall when planted in April 1873 to mark the fiftieth anniversary of Christian missionary work in Honolulu. By the mid-1960s, it stood over 65 feet high, with a 200-foot-wide canopy shading two-thirds of an acre.

Mitsumi's husband, Hirumi, was a horticulturist who once worked as a groundskeeper at the University of Hawaii. He loved to tell her stories about the banyan. With his hand holding her elbow, the couple walked past the banyan on their daily errands. While he guided her, people did not notice Mitsumi's limp, and she liked that.

"It's a kind of fig tree," he told her as they walked, dwarfed by the tree's vast canopy and tangled, vertical roots. "See those tendrils? They're actually the roots of tiny parasitic plants. The seeds grow high in the canopy. The saplings suck the life out of the host tree and turn into the tree's trunks."

"I think it's spooky." Mitsumi gazed at the many long, snarling limbs that stretched toward the earth from high above. "Looks like *Obaki*."

"No, it's not a ghost." Hirumi's light brown eyes twinkled. "In fact, the banyan holds special meaning to many people in the Pacific."

"Yes, yes. We all learned at the Hongwanji Buddhist Temple about how Lord Buddha sat under a banyan tree for seven days after his enlightenment." Mitsumi smiled, knowing more stories would follow.

"In Indonesia, people believe the tree is a symbol of unity and power, so much so that they put it on their national coat of arms." He went on. "The Hindu believe the gods and spirits of their ancestors linger under its shade. And in the Philippines, it is a home for good and evil spirits alike."

Mitsumi glanced toward the group of old men sitting deep in the shadows of the banyan. With nothing better to do, they staked their claim on wooden benches placed as close to its trunk as the bulging roots allowed. She shivered and grabbed Hirumi's arm.

"How can you be cold on this warm summer day?" Hirumi shook his head, laughed, and continued his story. "Even our own Princess Ka'iulani had a banyan tree. Her father, the Scottish businessman and horticulturist Archibald Scott Cleghorn, planted Hawaii's first banyan on the Princess's grand 'Āinahau Estate in Waikiki. It's gone now, replaced by a hotel, so sad. But because of our beautiful princess, you can find banyans on every one of our eight Hawaiian Islands."

Then he told her the old story about the Indian woman named Savitri, whose husband died as he was worshiping under a banyan tree. After his death, Savitri missed him so much she ventured into the realm of the dead to find him. There, under a banyan tree, she met Yama, the Lord of Death, and won her husband's life back.

"Till this day, women in India hold a ritual under banyan

trees on the first full moon in June to pray for the long and healthy lives of their husbands."

The wrinkles around Hirumi's smile curved up to his eyes.

"Dear wife, will you pray for my long life? Will you look for me in heaven after I die?"

Mitsumi shook her head. "You'll outlive me and you know it, and you won't find me praying under that tree!"

～

Now, Mitsumi wished she had prayed. Every day since Hirumi died thirteen months and fourteen days ago she walked by the banyan alone. She forced herself to get out, to shop, to live life's everyday journeys. When she arrived back at the house, she'd drop her bags and say to the quiet walls, "*Watashi wa ikiteiru.*" I am alive.

From her small, tidy home on Heliconia Place, Mitsumi walked by the banyan tree on her errands. It was the only path to the 'Aiea General Store, which was *makai*, or on the ocean side, of the tree. In the grocery section, she would buy fresh tofu and fish, and the crunchy watercress from Sumida Farms that she liked to put in her miso soup. In the back of the store was the lei stand, where the Hawaiian ladies saved stems of the best fresh flowers for Mitsumi's ikebana arrangements. She was such a regular that Mrs. Oshita, who ran the dry goods section, offered her a part-time job cutting fabric and selling notions weekdays from one to four.

She could not escape the tree, or the men in its shadows.

There, after years of toiling on their feet in the cane fields, the *Pinoy* sat. Their withered and wrinkled but still strong hands stretched taut under straightened elbows, fingers massaging thigh muscles that ached still. They argued politics, "talked story" about the old days, laughed, and watched people coming and going.

On a bright, hot day in early June, Mitsumi walked with eyes straight ahead over an even straighter backbone. From afar, she spied the men, who in fact were not much older than her sixty-five years. As she neared the shade of the tree, Mitsumi's stance changed. Her shoulders hunched, her face dropped, and her pace quickened.

It was worse when the one man called out to her, even if she couldn't see him, deep in the shade of the tree.

She frowned at the snickers, surmising their meaning even without knowing a word of the Filipino Tagalog language. The Bold One would call out in the local Pidgeon English dialect, "Ohhhhwee, dat is one berry fine-looking lady."

The other men laughed. Mitsumi turned her flushed face away and hurried on her way, her limp becoming more pronounced with each step.

As the days of the week passed, it got worse.

"Pppssss, ppsssss," the Bold One called, letting the saliva bubble under his tongue with the upper and lower teeth closed tight. It was a call well known throughout the islands. The locals called it the Filipino love call. It was a call of interest. A kind of, "I like talk to you." Or, "You turn me on." At its crudest, "I want to fuck your bones."

At the edge of the tree's shade, two men played chess. Patricio was a newcomer under the tree. He was lonely since the death of Momi, his wife of forty years, and his friend Motu invited him to join the group. "Come, we just 'talk story,'" he said, using the local euphemism for gossip. "But you no need talk. Just come." So, Patricio did.

Patricio looked up from the chessboard to study Mitsumi as she walked by late in the day, with satchels always topped by a few flowers. "She walks with such pride," Patricio said out loud. Motu watched his friend's face soften, and smiled.

~

On a hot June day in 1963, Mitsumi was on her way home. It had been a long week and her leg ached. She had finished her shift at the store and her arms were heavy with a bag of groceries topped by several stalks of red ginger, its showy seashell-shaped flowers bobbing. Her tanned skin glowed. She wished she hadn't forgotten her hat.

Tired and weary of the men and their words, she tried to ignore them. The laughter and the snickers pierced through the afternoon heat.

Then the Bold One called out to her. "Pppssss, ppsssss!"

Mitsumi's heart pounded. Sweat dripped between her breasts. Her bad leg tripped on a crack in the sidewalk. She fell forward onto Moanalua Road, scraping the palm of her right hand on the hot asphalt pavement to break her fall. The long flower spikes spilled onto the street, watercress and oranges tumbling behind.

Tires screeched. Men rushed from the shadows to help. The Bold One got to her first. As he reached out to Mitsumi, a strong hand caught his shoulder and threw him back onto the sidewalk. "Leave her alone." Patricio stood above him, eyes and face distorted, fists clenched. "Go back to the shadows where you belong, you, with your dirty, *pilau* mouth!"

The Bold One crawled backwards. The others hesitated.

"Get away, all of you." Patricio breathed to stop the shaking and compose himself.

He turned to Mitsumi and knelt beside her. "Sit, sit. Rest . . . Are you okay?" he said in perfect Japanese. He hesitated, then touched her arm. "Please, let me help you."

"Eh?" Mitsumi pulled her arm back, then turned toward him, confused and startled by the light brown eyes that somehow looked so familiar. She sat, embarrassed, on the side of Moanalua Road, buses and cars whizzing past, with this stranger kneeling beside her, offering her his arm.

As she regained her composure, Patricio picked up the groceries from the sweltering pavement. When he returned to her side, he saw her hand was bleeding, then knelt and placed the bags on the ground. He reached into his shirt pocket and handed her a folded, clean white handkerchief. She blinked, took the hanky, and thanked him. *"Arigatou gozaimasu."*

"Dou itashimashite." He told her she was welcome.

How can this Filipino man speak Japanese so well? she wondered. He wasn't like the others under the tree.

"Are you sure you can walk? Perhaps sit a while longer? There's a bench . . ." He nodded toward the tree.

"Īe! Īe! She shook her head side to side.

"Can I call you a taxi, or perhaps walk you to your home?"

"Īe . . . no." Mitsumi's eyes narrowed as her hand massaged her brow.

She studied his face and wondered why he looked so familiar and why she felt protected with him by her side. Curious why she felt comforted by his presence, like they were old friends, she struggled for words. Tears came into her eyes.

Patricio reached out.

"Please, may I help you carry your groceries to your house? I won't go to your door . . . only make sure you make it home okay . . . We'll go slow." Patricio paused and looked her in the eye and lowered his chin. "I mean no harm."

With her groceries still in his hands, Mitsumi looked back toward the tree, nodded at Patricio, and took his hand to rise. She turned toward Heliconia Place.

After a few steps, she stopped and looked back at the tree. Her eyes narrowed. She inhaled and straightened her shoulders. Without saying a word, she walked into the depths of the tree. The Bold One stood up. Before he could say anything, Mitsumi slapped him across his face with her bleeding palm. He fell back into the bench. All eyes turned to Mitsumi.

"No more," she said firmly in English. Slowly, she looked at each of them, her eyes finally resting on the Bold One. "No more."

The wind whispered as leaves rained down. A ray of sunshine broke from behind a cloud and danced through the banyan's canopy. Mitsumi looked up, then walked back to Patricio in the sun. He smiled and took her arm. Over the Ko'olau mountains, a pale, full moon rose in the early summer sky.

9

NEUROTIC BEAUTY - LADAN MURPHY

J oseph and Martha loved the Brekenwood mansion the moment they set eyes on it. Joseph knew the true value of the ruined building beneath the peeled paint, crooked wood frame, piles of dust and spiderwebs. Martha imagined enjoying her afternoon tea, watching the Pacific Ocean from behind the bay windows. They purchased the charming nine-teenth-century Victorian mansion on a cliff overlooking the Pacific Ocean in northern California. They invested their time and money to renovate it to an eight-bedroom B&B and brought it back to its original glory.

The B&B's large front door opened to an inviting foyer, leading to a cozy great hall and a sunny breakfast nook. The wooden spiral staircase in the middle led to the bedrooms on the second story. The wicker chairs and tables in the back courtyard provided a relaxing open-air, ocean-view area surrounded by rosebushes and trees.

Martha couldn't but hold her breath when she recovered a framed painting of the early owners, Irma and William Breken-wood, from the attic. William sat on an armchair in his navy-blue uniform, his thick groomed mustache curled and twisted all the way to his ears, his arm reaching to hold his wife's with a look of longing on his face. Irma sat by his chair on the ground in an ivory lace dress, which spread widely on the red carpet. Her wavy, light brown hair draped to her waist, her arms stretched to reach his, and her long fingers lightly brushed against his arms. The painting hung proudly in the great hall where it had so long ago.

Legend had it that in the early twentieth century, Irma William R. Brekenwood, the beautiful and charming eighteen-year-old bride of the handsome thirty-five-year-old captain, William R. Brekenwood, died of a broken heart in the mansion soon after having lost her husband in a shipwreck in the tumultuous sea. Ever since Irma's passing, her ghost sat on the window ledge in her bedroom on full-moon nights, looking out to the ocean. Her long hair danced in the breeze, her eyes browsed the horizon, her lips shivered as she sang softly and cried at her misfortunes to the roar of the breaking waves on the shore.

The mansion was then left to Miss Jane Moozi, the housekeeper who lived there until her death 60 years later at the age of 85. Miss Jane's dried-up body was found with eyes wide open in the great hall.

Martha and Joseph renamed the Brekenwood mansion Irma's B&B. Deservedly so, since Irma's ghost attracted many ghost chasers, making it a success. The tours of Irma's room took place during the day, while she was left to her misery at night to perform for her adoring fans. She mesmerized the guests when she appeared on the balcony in her white lacy dress, swaying and singing. The pilgrimage of enthusiasts and other travelers kept Martha and Joseph busy. But they often took time to sit by the bay window, enjoying their afternoon tea, reading the local newspaper, to keep abreast of ghostly news.

~

"'Irma's B&B, a real ghost chaser's paradise or fancy trickery?'"

Joseph read aloud as he put his teacup on the table. "Who is this Ms. Tisdale writing about our B&B in *The Abnormal*?" he asked.

"Another reporter trying to make a name for herself at our expense," Martha said.

Joseph devised a plan to stop the reporter trying to destroy the business in which they had invested so much of their time and their life.

"We should invite her to stay here and show her some hospitality," Joseph said.

So, Ms. Tisdale received and accepted an invitation to Irma's B&B.

Martha had a bad feeling about the whole deal from the moment she set eyes on the woman standing in the great hall. Ms. Tisdale stood in her pantsuit with her dark hair pulled up tightly, looking around curiously through a big-framed pair of glasses. Her nose pulled upward as if she were about to break the biggest story in the history of the Ghost Chasers Community. Her hosts, Martha and Joseph, graciously escorted her to a second-story, ocean-view room next to Irma's. Joseph smiled, confident all doubts would be put to rest once Ms. Tisdale experienced Irma's sweet singing firsthand.

Martha and Joseph stayed in their room, waiting for the moonlight and the sound of crashing waves to do their magic, but the night of smooth songs didn't happen. Ms. Tisdale, unimpressed by the uneventful night, sat at the breakfast table the next morning triumphantly.

"A ghost should be a ghost and act like a ghost. This is just disappointing," she said.

Martha's bad feeling persisted, so she was not surprised to hear what Joseph read her from the next issue of *The Abnormal*.

"Mrs. Irma Brekenwood, a no-show at her full-moon singing event? Is this town being duped or is Irma having a night off?"

"How did this happen? Irma has never missed a full moon, clear or cloudy, yet now she's gone shy at the sight of Ms. Tisdale?" Martha sobbed.

"We have to do something; this isn't good for business.

Maybe printing the testimonies of our past guests can prove Irma is genuine." Joseph scratched his head.

Martha felt her blood boiling.

"This can't be good for business!" Martha cried. "Is that all you think about? What happened to my sweet Irma? What did that woman do to her?"

Irma sat on the window ledge, pouting, that night.

"Here are some lilies for you, darling, your favorite," Martha said to the ghost she had come to love and who had become much more than an attraction for their business.

∽

Although the usual pilgrims continued making their visit, negative press discouraged new customers.

Joseph took out a full-page advertisement filled with the happy guests' testimonies in *The Abnormal*. He hoped it would stir up excitement in the ghost-chasing community, since the number of new guests had dwindled after Ms. Tisdale's taunting articles.

The couple designed perfect ghostly getaway packages for their regulars and potential new customers. One April night, the moonlit water glittered, the waves played their music, and the gentle breeze engulfed the patrons snuggling by the fire in the courtyard, watching Irma singing from her bedroom.

"Believers or hallucinators?" the next article from Ms. Tisdale read.

Joseph thought about extending a follow-up invitation to Ms. Tisdale, but the idea made Martha cringe.

"She is taunting us. I am not having it," Martha sneered.

"This is our retirement, our business—we should approach it logically," Joseph said.

So, Joseph convinced Martha to accept the plan, with the condition that Ms. Tisdale witness the performance from the courtyard and agree not to bully or make fun of Irma. Irma was to be left to her misery at night without intimidation or harassment.

Once again, Joseph extended an invitation and Ms. Tisdale accepted.

Joseph and Martha squeezed each other's hands, watching from the courtyard with Ms. Tisdale next to them, while Irma's light silhouette appeared at her bedroom balcony and started singing. No reporter could dispute such overwhelming evidence. They slept well that night.

"Not so innocent! Irma bullied Ms. Jane for years and eventually scared her to death, the grandniece claims," Miss Tisdale's next article read.

The article cited the grandniece of the former housekeeper, who claimed her aunt had suffered at the hands of Irma the ghost for over half a century.

"Is she serious? Now, she's smearing Irma." Joseph tossed the newspaper on the table with dismay.

"I told you so," Martha uttered through her teeth. "Nothing good comes out of us dealing with that woman. I didn't trust her from the moment I saw her."

"What nonsense!" Joseph shook his head, thinking about the article.

"You called her back, you let this nosy reporter in our business, and now you have ruined it all," Martha said, tearing up.

Joseph reached for her hand and held it in his, reassuring her he would take care of the problem. He delved into his damage control sense and tried to calmly evaluate the situation. He paid a visit to his lawyer and realized there was nothing he could do legally. The lawyer suggested a civil talk with the reporter might do the trick. Joseph called Ms. Tisdale but kept his usual calm voice. She was anything but apologetic. He could picture Ms. Tisdale's pulled-up nose and prideful eyes in his mind.

"It is my job to show every side and every angle," she claimed.

"Well, it doesn't seem you show Irma's side at all," Joseph responded.

"This may have some truth in it and I am willing to write Irma's side of the story, but I have to write the truth and not what you want me to write."

"That is all we ask for," Joseph finished on a positive note.

Joseph reported back to Martha.

"We shall see! I don't put anything past that woman." Martha shrugged and knew soon she would be saying, *I told you so!*

~

The full moon—the busiest night of the month—was approaching; the B&B's phone rang off the hook and every rooms was booked. All was well, and Martha enjoyed how Ms. Tisdale unwittingly had given Irma a new dimension. The unpleasant articles seemed irrelevant now, and Ms. Tisdale was left off the guest list intentionally.

The night was filled with excitement. Moonlight shone on the fans in the courtyard, waves crashed on the shore in the background, and Irma began to sing. The wind carried the muffled sound of a woman talking from the balcony, annoying the guests in the courtyard. Irma stopped singing and cried a little before disappearing. Martha ran to the room to ask the woman to hush up; the room closest to Irma's—the most expensive room—came with a no-harassment policy. Irma was to be left in peace! When Martha reached the base of the stairs, a blond woman with heavy makeup, blue jeans, and a long shirt was running hurriedly down the staircase. Martha pulled to the side and let her pass, and within seconds Irma came floating behind the fleeing woman.

The guests in the courtyard whispered about Irma's interrupted singing; the sound of objects being thrown and commotion drew some of the guests to the great hall. They watched the woman, now with a tilted blond wig—which was about to fall off—being chased by Irma, passing them, and heading for the courtyard. After circling the courtyard, she ran back to the house, heading for the door. Before she could get there, she fell on her back in the great hall.

"Do you want to get scared to death too?" Irma floated over her, face to face, as the woman panted and used her elbows to move backwards.

"Ms. Tisdale? What the . . .!" Martha shouted at the woman, unable to finish.

Irma flew up toward the wooden bookshelf. Dust spread in the trail of a book falling from the shelf. Joseph caught and opened the dusty book.

"*Diary of Jane Moozi,*" Joseph said, reading the title. The musty smell of old paper filled the air as he opened the aged yellowish diary. "'Irma, the silly girl runs around the house with her puffy dresses like a five-year-old child. Little does she know she is no match for me. I have her husband in the palm of my hand. Soon she will be gone and everything of hers becomes mine—her husband, her house. I'll make sure of that. A man's crown may be his wife, but his lover is the gemstone set on the crown.'"

"Wooh, that was way cool, the best ever!" Eighteen-year-old Timmy, a returning guest traveling with his family, cheered as he kept clicking his camera phone button. His praise didn't go unrewarded: Irma turned and smiled at him.

~

"'Is Irma, the forever beauty, sweet and innocent, or a scary and mean ghost?'" Joseph read from the next issue of *The Abnormal.* Martha smiled.

She'd decided it was her turn to find the next step. After all, Joseph's way hadn't exactly gone well.

Timmy's picture of Irma chasing Ms. Tisdale on Instagram sparked a following and shot Irma to the top favorite ghost in the Ghost Chasers Community.

Irma was in great spirit; she'd decided it was time to stop mourning her lost life. Her husband's infidelity and his mistress's tale of betrayal were bygones now. Miss Jane had paid dearly for poisoning Irma and blaming her death on a broken heart.

Ms. Tisdale learned the best way to stay relevant and win the Ghost Chasers News Award was to stay on the good side of the liberated neurotic ghost and the holder of the diary, which provided a wealth of information that would keep the ghostly news going.

10

HERE LYES BURIED - JENNIFER M. FRANKS

R ockwell Baylor liked it when they died from disease. Then he could carve a skull over crossed bones into their gravestone, or an hourglass, as a reminder that life was fleeting. A skull with wings was another favorite, showing the ultimate triumph of death. Life could end at any moment—as it had been doing lately in Boston.

He chiseled the words: *Here lyes buried the body of Rupert Adams, Died March 9th 1698, aged 17 years, 2 months and 5 days.* The flat, gray stone had a rounded top, as they all did. *Who decided to make them rounded?* he wondered. At two feet wide by three feet tall and four inches thick, more words would fit if it was rectangular. Like most things, he couldn't make sense of it. He hadn't known Rupert, but his older brother Samuel had.

Samuel said Rupert had died a horrible death after stepping on a rusted nail. His whole body had gone rigid a few days later. His jaws clamped shut and his last cry muffled through teeth clenched into a grin that wasn't a grin at all.

Rockwell put his initials behind the gravestone so his father could see his work. Already three rows in the cemetery were his and he was proud of them. His father said his work was better than Samuel's. Father had taught his sons everything he knew about stone cutting that he had learned from Grandfather. Some of Grandfather's gravestones were so old they were sinking in the earth and didn't sit straight anymore. In his day, they didn't allow pictures—only names and dates—on the stones. Rockwell was happy the Puritan ways had ended and that he was a better artist than Samuel.

Samuel was good at everything and he had teeth that lined up straight. All the girls liked him. Sometimes Rockwell followed the girls home and hid in the shadows, peeking in at them through the windows. They always brushed their hair before a looking glass, plaiting it before they put on their sleep caps and blew out the candles in their rooms.

Someone was crying in the shop. It was a sound he heard often. Rockwell put down the chisel and mallet and went to see who it was, because Father and Samuel were gone. A girl wearing a black cloak was crying into a handkerchief. Her long red hair spilled out from under her hood.

"Can I help you, miss?" Rockwell asked.

Her hands fell away from her face, revealing watery blue eyes and rosy cheeks wet with tears.

"I need a gravestone," she said in a trembling voice. "Is Samuel here?" she looked past Rockwell, glancing around the shop.

"Samuel went to Lexington with our father today." Rockwell felt his heart beating in his chest. He looked down at his boots; it was hard to look into her sad, pretty eyes. "But I can help you. Who is it for?" he asked when he managed to look up at her again.

"My father," the girl replied gravely. "He died of fever."

"I know the fever's been fierce this winter. I'm sorry."

She nodded, fighting back a fresh wave of sobs.

"What was his name?"

"Joseph," she replied, "Joseph Watley. He was forty-eight years old on Tuesday."

"When is the service?"

"In the morning. I know I'm not leaving you much time—it just happened so suddenly and I didn't have anyone that could help me . . . My father and my uncle are all the family I had left."

"I can have it ready for you by morning, ma'am. Up at King's Chapel Cemetery?"

"Yes," she replied, her eyes filling again with tears.

"And where do you live?"

She looked a little surprised by this but answered, wiping away a traveling tear with her glove. "Just beyond the Old North Church."

"Don't worry, Miss, I'll take care of it. Your name is?" he prodded gently, trying not to appear too eager.

"Agnes." She looked confused. "I'm sorry, what was your name?"

"Rockwell. I'll be at the cemetery first thing in the morning, Miss Agnes."

"Thank you. You've been very kind. Samuel didn't tell me he had a little brother."

Rockwell tensed and his brow furrowed. "Sometimes he forgets to mention it."

"I'm not sure when I can pay you . . ." she started to say, not listening to him.

"Don't worry about that now, Miss Agnes. Let's get your father a proper burial."

"Thank you," she replied, her blue eyes brighter in their pool of tears. She left and Rockwell watched her go. Then he picked a blank gravestone and carved a winged skull for Mr. Watley, chiseling in his name and date of death below it. After sundown, he closed the shop and went to find where Miss Agnes lived.

~

Rockwell found the house where Agnes lived fairly easily. Like she said, it was just behind the Old North Church. Cloaked in darkness, he felt safe enough to peer into the only room with light glowing through lace curtains. Agnes sat before a scowling man, shaking her head *no*. He pounded his fist against the table and she flinched. He pointed his finger at her and shouted something Rockwell couldn't discern. Her pale blue eyes welled like a pond in spring, brimming until tears cascaded down her cheeks. Her red hair flowed along the black bodice of her mourning dress like tongues of fire from Bible stories. The man left Agnes, and Rockwell could see the light of his oil lamp bouncing down a hallway as he made his way to a far room in the house. Agnes breathed heavily, as if she had been holding her breath for a long while and needed to catch up. She roughly wiped at tears with the back of her hand, then abruptly turned her gaze to the window. Instinctively, Rockwell stepped aside. There was no way she could see him in the dark, but she must have sensed his heavy stare. When he peered in again, Agnes had a lantern in her hand and was headed for the stairs.

Annoyed, Rockwell saw an upper room illuminate. How would he see her up there? Should he sneak inside the church and find an upstairs window? Too risky. An old maple tree nearby offered a better solution. Rockwell climbed it and positioned himself on a wide branch where he could watch Agnes in her room, brushing her hair slowly near the window. He smiled. This was what he wanted to see.

On the ground, a shadow approached, tossing a pebble against her window. Agnes startled, put down her brush and ran from the room, leaving behind her oil lamp. Rockwell became annoyed. Moments later, Agnes was outside in a dark cloak. "Samuel," she whispered.

"Over here," came a reply from behind the shrubs beneath the tree.

Agnes ran to him and they embraced. "Oh Samuel! It's horrible! My Uncle Jessop says I have to marry right away! He's already arranged a betrothal!"

"Marry whom?" Samuel demanded.

"The blacksmith, Mr. Adler!"

"The widower?"

"Yes! Samuel, what can be done?" she cried, burying her face in his shoulder.

Samuel stroked her hair. "Don't worry, we'll make a plan. You will not be marrying that old goat. I'll see you tomorrow at the cemetery. Don't argue with your uncle—we'll make it right somehow." Samuel kissed Agnes and they parted ways.

Rockwell stayed in the tree long after Agnes blew out her lamp and her room went dark. He lay on his back along a sturdy branch and let his legs dangle over the sides. Through the barren branches of the tree, he could see countless stars and watch the vapor of his breath rise to meet them. It was getting cold. Two thoughts occupied his mind: anger that his brother had come, and his need to help beautiful, pitiful Agnes.

"Rockwell, how long are you going to stay up in that tree?" Agnes called from below.

Rockwell caught his breath and became very still. *How did she know I was here?* His mind raced.

"Well, are you going to come down or freeze to death?"

Rockwell found the courage to look down at her. She was still wearing her cloak, and her pale face under the black hood looked disembodied, like a ghost in the darkness.

"I was just about to come down, Miss Agnes," Rockwell replied nervously.

"Good. Because I need you to help me with something."

Rockwell dropped down from the lowest branch of the tree. He was relieved that she didn't ask him why he had been there in the first place, but maybe she'd guessed.

"Follow me into the house and be really quiet," she demanded. Rockwell nodded awkwardly and did as he was told. She did not hold an oil lamp. Whatever they were doing, Agnes wanted it to be secret.

They reached a closed door in the far corner of the house, where her uncle had gone earlier. No lamplight illuminated the door frame. Agnes turned to Rockwell, her face very serious. "Can you keep a secret?" He nodded. He liked Agnes sharing a secret with him.

"Good. Help me carry my Uncle Jessop to the barn."

Rockwell followed Agnes through the door. "Did he fall?" he asked.

"Yes."

Inside, Rockwell saw that her uncle was wrapped in sheets.

"You carry one end and I'll carry the other," she said calmly.

When Rockwell lifted his end, a lifeless arm fell from the sheets. A shiver ran up his spine. "Don't ask questions, just help me take him to the barn," Agnes said sternly.

Rockwell felt light-headed, but he did as she commanded.

They carried the body quietly through the house, out the door, and to the barn nearby. The horses watched them warily and sidestepped as they passed.

"Let's put him here." Agnes motioned to a place right behind a Clydesdale horse. They dropped Uncle Jessop's body and Rockwell wiped off the cold sweat that was beading up on his forehead.

Agnes went to work quickly. She rolled her uncle out of the sheets and pulled a bottle of liquor from a satchel she wore over her shoulder. She poured it over her uncle's shirt and a little in his mouth, setting the bottle in the crook of his arm. Next, she took a mallet and horseshoe and crouched over her uncle's dead body, placing the horseshoe against his forehead. Looking up, she said, "Look away, Rockwell."

Rockwell looked to the right just as the sound of the mallet struck the horseshoe with a loud *clink!*

"All right, let's go," Agnes said, tossing the horseshoe into the haystack behind them. Rockwell could see a horseshoe impression on her dead uncle's forehead. *Clever girl!*

Outside, she faced him, kissing him briefly on the cheek. "I'll see you at my father's funeral tomorrow?"

"Sure," Rockwell replied. He didn't feel right about things, but she had kissed him, and that made him weak in the knees.

"Don't forget to keep our secret."

"I won't, Miss Agnes."

~

Miss Agnes sobbed bitterly at her father's funeral. A small group assembled at the graveside, their faces long with sorrow for her. The pastor said Joseph Watley was a good man and mentioned that poor Agnes had no family left. Her Uncle Jessop, in his sorrow, had taken to drink and had suffered a dreadful mishap the night before.

"Got kicked in the head by a horse," one elderly woman whispered loudly to another. Both women shook their heads sadly.

Rockwell didn't look Agnes in the eyes, but he felt the weight of her occasional stare in his direction. When the service ended, he and Samuel shoveled dirt into the open grave. The gravedigger was digging another hole nearby for Uncle Jessop. Clumps of cold earth thudded against the wood of Mr. Watley's casket, scattering over the sides until the valleys around it filled in. The casket began to shrink from view, and Agnes let out a cry of lamentation with every shovel of earth that buried her father.

Behind his grave stood the headstone Rockwell had carved for him. He would need to carve another for Uncle Jessop later today. What would he choose for his gravestone? Rockwell wondered. An hourglass that counted down time until his niece killed him? A skull and crossed bones for poison? How had she done it? She seemed so small and fragile. There had been no blood on his body. Rockwell leaned against his shovel, catching his breath. Carelessly, he let his eyes wander and they met with the bloodshot eyes of Agnes. For the brief second, hers narrowed, and Rockwell quickly looked away. He started shoveling again. He decided he wasn't going to watch Agnes in her room that night. He didn't like that they shared a secret anymore.

~

Here lyes buried the body of Jessop Watley, aged about 54. Rockwell chiseled the date of his death on the gravestone, then blew away the stone fragments that cluttered the letters. Uncle Jessop got the hourglass rather than the grinning skull. It seemed fitting to Rockwell. As he was finishing his work, a young man entered the shop. Samuel spoke to him for a while and came away with an order.

"Who is it for?" Rockwell asked.

"The blacksmith, Mr. Adler."

Rockwell felt a lump in his throat. Swallowing hard, he asked, "And . . . what was the cause of death?"

"Sounds like it was an accident. He got impaled by a fire poker while he was smelting. He must have fallen back upon it."

Rockwell had difficulty breathing.

"Are you all right?" Samuel asked him.

"Just one of my breathing fits again."

"You haven't had a fit in a long time," Samuel replied. "Why don't you take a break? I'll finish up."

∼

That evening, Rockwell found his mother's Bible in her sewing basket beside her bed, where she had always kept it. It had been years since she died, but nobody had changed the way she kept the house. Her Sunday dresses were still folded in a trunk, and her hairbrush sat dusty on the vanity next to a butterfly clip she used to wear in her hair.

Rockwell took her Bible and went to his room. He felt like reading something spiritual. He closed his eyes and opened it, deciding whatever page he landed on, he would read from. *Judges 16.* Rockwell began to read about Samson and Delilah. The conniving woman tried three times to learn the source of Samson's power. He finally confessed his power lay in his long hair. She betrayed his trust and cut his hair while he slept. His power lost, Delilah handed him over to the Philistines, who blinded him. He was mocked and unable to defend himself.

Samson wanted revenge, yet he was remorseful. Samson prayed to God for mercy and his hair began to grow back.

A clinking noise against the window startled Rockwell. Another *clink* followed. *Pebbles*, he was certain of it. He closed the Bible and slowly went to look out the window. A bright half-moon cast shadows from trees on the empty lawn below. One tree moved. Instinctively, Rockwell stepped away from the window. He leaned with his back against the wall and held his hand over his heart. Another pebble pinged the glass and he heard his name.

"Rockwell, come down and talk with me." Agnes called his name again—louder this time.

Everything told him not to go outside to meet her. While he was thinking of what to do, she called his name once more. Frustrated, he appeared before the window, holding up a hand that said he'd be down in a minute.

As Rockwell walked quietly down the hallway, he noticed Samuel wasn't in his bedroom. Strange, because he had gone to bed early, claiming fatigue from digging in the frostbitten earth. Father's door was closed and no amber light traced his door frame. He wasn't up reading like he usually was. Rockwell slipped on his boots, grabbed his coat, and opened the door. Whatever Agnes wanted, he wasn't going to do it. He didn't like Miss Agnes anymore.

Outside, Agnes rushed toward him and Rockwell was forced to put his arms around her. She cried into his chest, "Oh, Rockwell! I wallow in anguish!"

He held her loosely, carefully choosing his words. "Anyone would after burying their father."

"But you wouldn't even look at me today," she accused, gazing up at him.

"I'm sorry, Miss Agnes." He tried not to look in her eyes, so she couldn't cast a Delilah spell over him. "I was digging."

"You added to my grief."

His arms tensed around her.

"You shouldn't have done that," she added.

Rockwell caught his breath as a sudden pain seared through his abdomen. It splintered like the lightning bolts he loved to watch in summer storms. You never knew if a bolt would stretch across the sky or dip down to the earth. Sometimes, if you were lucky, a bolt would strike a tree, splitting it in half. The pain shot down his legs, across his torso, up his spine and around his shoulders. Dropping his arms, Rockwell staggered backward. Looking down, he could see the handle and end of a silver blade glinting in the moonlight. The rest of the dagger was embedded in his flesh. A stream of warm blood shot up his throat and into his mouth, making him sputter. "Why?" he rasped.

"You weren't going to keep our secret," she replied, "I could tell."

Rockwell dropped to his knees, clinging to his stomach and wincing through fresh waves of pain. "But I did . . ."

"Pray tell me, where is Samuel?" she asked, looking up at the dark house.

Rockwell fought the sensation to lie down for a minute and rest. If he did, he knew he might never rise again. "Samuel isn't home," he muttered, after spitting out more blood. He had to save his brother from her.

"He isn't home? Where can he be at this late hour, I wonder?"

Rockwell doubled over, his forehead touching the cold earth. Memories swirled through his mind. He saw his mother smiling at him, his father teaching him how to cut stone, and he saw himself chasing Samuel through a field. *I just need to close my eyes and rest*, he thought. *Just for a moment . . .*

A light flashed from the darkness as the piercing *bang* of a rifle rang out. Miss Agnes collapsed beside Rockwell. She didn't cry, nor did she writhe in pain. She simply stared at him in horror, breathing heavily until her eyes became fixed and lifeless.

Samuel and Father were at his side, telling him to hold on. Telling him to fight. Samuel dropped his rifle and embraced his brother, rocking him gently. Mother came too, surrounded by a great light. She was reaching for her son, but then she started crying.

◁

Here Lyes Buried the body of Rockwell Baylor, Born December 4, 1683 Died March 11, 1698 aged 15 years, three months and seven days. A winged angel was etched above his name. Samuel and Father wept quietly at his graveside. Neighbors surrounded them, as did many of Mother's friends from church. They couldn't see Rockwell standing there, observing his gravestone and the mound of loosely packed dirt over his casket.

Across the cemetery was another fresh mound of dirt. Miss Agnes sat alone, staring bleakly at her gravestone. She wore her dark cloak, like she usually did. Her gravestone was a small, stone plaque. Rockwell guessed that Samuel and Father hadn't taken the time to carve an image for hers, or given her a costly stone.

Agnes finally looked up and noticed Rockwell. Rising slowly, she walked over to him, her body passing through gravestones in her path like she was made of smoke.

"Are you ready?" she said faintly, her pale blue eyes greatly saddened.

"Yes," Rockwell replied.

Together they left the cemetery, disappearing for a moment. When they reappeared, they were at Miss Agnes's house behind the Old North Church. Agnes went inside and stared wanly out the window of her bedroom, slowly brushing her hair. Rockwell climbed the tree and sat on the limb, where he could watch the living below. Every night after dark, he met Miss Agnes in the house, and they'd walk together to the barn, carrying her Uncle Jessop's dead body. This was their punishment for all eternity.

Once, a living little boy could see them and screamed . . . but that was two hundred years after Rockwell and Agnes lyed buried in the cemetery.

11

ADRIATIC - ANDREA CARTER

L ooking out the airplane window, Leslie searched for the city of Venice. Instead she saw pictures of people at Carnevale dressed up in gold and blue costumes and white mouthless masks in the magazine on her lap. She blinked to make sure she had not missed the Adriatic. The flight pattern on-screen indicated the plane would land in view of that body of water, but she only saw green and yellow patchwork farm fields under the white wispy clouds.

"Almost like home," she said to Mark and tried to shrug off the disappointment. She had wanted to go to Venice ever since an Italian exchange student she met at nursing school described the canals, hidden streets, and secret staircases.

They were on their honeymoon.

Mark barely took a look. At six feet four inches tall, he could easily see over Leslie's head. A thick lock of ginger hair covered his left eye.

"Nah," said Mark, putting the earbud back in his ear. He continued to nod to the music playing on his cell phone.

"I sure don't see Venice," she said, staring out the window again. Then she glanced down at the magazine and picked up the story she had been reading about how during Carnevale in the thirteenth century, people put on masks and did things they weren't supposed to do.

"Anything to throw away?" The blond flight attendant came down the aisle asking for trash and swished a cellophane bag back and forth for people to toss in their used cups, cans, and napkins. She wore dark red lipstick, and her teeth were porcelain-tile perfect when she smiled.

"What would you like?" asked Mark, grinning.

"What have you got?" the attendant shot back.

Leslie watched Mark pretend to take off his wedding ring. His blue-green eyes glinted at the attendant.

The attendant looked at Mark and sucked in her lower lip.

"When can we actually *see* Venice?" asked Leslie. She forced a smile at the attendant and re-coiled her thick mass of long, dirty-blond hair into a bun, but her shoulders were tense and holding the unnatural smile started to hurt.

∿

When they had met ten months ago, Mark was still with his old girlfriend. He always got people's attention, tall and lanky, a confident storyteller, his eyes the color of glacial runoff, a blue or green or both. There was something in those eyes that could cut the hardest rock. Leslie was new in town, had just earned her RN and left Eugene to get away from her parents—and get away from the guy she broke up with, who got too high and kept borrowing money from her. Her friend Maria invited her to be on the neighborhood softball team. Leslie protested. She wasn't much of an athlete, but Maria said they played for the beer after the games. The beer and the boys.

One night, Mark sat next to her at the brewery after a game. He ran a solar panel business serving residential clients, and soon commercial buildings. He drove a truck with a Sierra Club bumper sticker. Leslie apologized for letting the last home run from the other team get past her in center field. She was not that great at throwing. Mark took off his baseball cap, and she could see his eyes. He told her not to worry about it. He told her they were all there for the fun.

"You do like to have fun, don't you?" he asked. She felt herself blush all the way down to her ankles.

At the next softball game, he told her he had broken up with his girlfriend and asked her to go out with him. "I really want to get to know you."

Snowmelt gushed through her bloodstream; every seeded wildflower bloomed.

"You want *me*?" she asked, and then she laughed nervously. "That didn't come out right."

"It came out just fine." His eyes were like rushing water that could take out trees, boulders, feet of riverbank.

But right before they married, he'd flirted with someone at the bar who was on the other team. When Leslie mentioned it, he told her she was insecure. She said it hurt. He said it hurt because she had it in her head to think he was flirting. She was hurting herself. The woman was one of his clients. He just liked to talk to people.

"You're right," she apologized afterward.

"Your old boyfriend sure primed you for sad shit," he said.

∾

When they touched down on the runway, Leslie realized she'd completely missed seeing Venice. Once in the vast, vaulted airport waiting area, Mark stopped at the nearest stone bench to look up the water taxi. He parked his roller suitcase, took his phone out of his shorts pocket, and scrolled the screen. Leslie peeled off her backpack; her T-shirt was already damp with sweat. She unzipped the pack and changed from her running shoes into sandals. The open arcade where they stood echoed with people speaking Italian a mile a minute. She thought about the blond flight attendant.

"You with me?" Mark grabbed his suitcase handle.

Leslie looked at her wedding ring. Mark was just being himself. How could she doubt him? She needed to be more trusting. They followed the stream of people through the automatic doors of the airport terminal and headed down to the water bus station. They were still far away from Venice.

"We jump in one of these vaporettos, and it takes us all the way to the Lido."

"I still don't see why we couldn't stay in Venice," said Leslie.

"Nothing was available, babe. But I promise, we'll see everything in Venice. We're here for a week. Look, we'll go to the B&B, put our stuff away, and eat. Then we'll come back." Sweat beaded on his forehead and upper lip.

The vaporetto sped through the water swells. Leslie stared at the hints of shapes appearing along the horizon. Finally, she could see a tower before they headed into the Grand Canal. Leslie pointed out St. Mark's, and the hooded vertical eyes of the mansions that rose like rescued drowning victims, rows and rows of them, bony, ornate, and pastel. She had only imagined Venice. But this was the real thing. A few cats lazed in the sun on the docks. She tried to point out the Hotel Danieli, its Middle Eastern fortress façade keeping all its sensual secrets hidden in brocade and marble. Mark stared at his phone.

"It doesn't seem real, does it?" She nudged him.

He nodded, bobbing his head up and down.

They hustled up the gangplank once they got to the Lido dock. The weight of Leslie's backpack shifted back and forth.

"We catch the regular bus on the next street," he yelled to her over his shoulder. In a matter of seconds Mark was way ahead of her, his head high above everyone else. She tried to yell at him, but maneuvering with the clumsy backpack made it hard for her to be heard. Four cats slinked in front of her into the shade of a bush next to a yellow house. She fought off the sleepiness, dehydration, and impatience, half-skipping, half-running to catch him.

"Hey, I'm not as fast a mover as you," she panted behind him as they boarded the bus.

"I thought you wanted to make it back to Venice."

"I do, but could you wait up?" said Leslie.

They shuffled past the seated passengers, and the bus took off with unexpected speed. Leslie tried to grab one of the plastic straps to stand, but instead she fell back against Mark.

"God, you have no coordination," he laughed.

The bus stopped. Leslie followed Mark as he pressed through the Italians getting out the rear door. He went trucking way out in front of her again, and she broke into an uneven run, stumbling after him as he went across the street, down an alley. Her sandals slapped the pavement. She thought of those spy movies set in Europe where there's always a chase on a red-tiled roof and someone winds up dead in a fountain. The faster she tried to run, the more the backpack sent her in a zigzag motion.

The light at the next street turned red, and cars honked and tires screeched. She waved at the people in their cars who raised their voices. A fist came out of one of the car windows. She tried to apologize but made it worse by stopping to say she was sorry. She saw Mark in an open plaza area with a terra-cotta fountain and ran toward him, her sandals landing hard on the asphalt, the concrete, the dirt, until she stood in front of him. A white cat sunned itself on the fountain wall.

Mark pointed to the B&B. It was a row home, the end unit, pale pink stucco with a red roof. A blue-and-white-striped awning looked like an eyelid above the balcony of their room on the second floor. A ceiling fan whirred, and the French doors to the balcony were open. The interior colors were those of Rubenesque nudes. The gauze curtains looked like fish gills. The awning stretched over the balcony and offered shade. A lounging gray cat raised its head and looked at Leslie with its yellow eyes. She noticed one of the cat's ears had a tiny triangle cut out at the edge.

Mark took off his shirt and patted himself dry with the two hand towels left out for them on the little desk outside the bathroom. He stood with the balcony doors wide open. Leslie dug through the backpack to put on shorts. Since the bathroom had no room for her toiletry bag, she opened the larger bottom drawer of the desk to stow it there. Silk scarves filled the drawer. She grabbed at them, but they were wrapped around something that fell out.

"Oh, wow." She stepped back.

It was a black half-mask, leather, a cat face with wide pointed ears. The eye holes angled up, and the exaggerated furrows of the brow line made it look like there was a giant arrow between the eyes.

"Wild," said Leslie.

"What's up?" Mark turned around and saw her holding the mask.

She held it up to her face, the crumbly leather underside touching her cheeks. There was a faint perfume infused in the leather smell; it was almost like she could smell the face of whoever had worn it. She turned it back around and held it at arm's length.

"Someone must have left this," said Leslie.

"Don't get weird on me." Mark looked over her shoulder at it.

"Oh, you think I'll turn into some hot S&M chick or something."

"No, that will never happen to you," he laughed. "Anyway, I need to eat. You stay if you want to," he said.

Leslie wanted to say something.

"Wait, don't move." He kissed her lips, her neck.

His hands dug at her shorts to feel her waist. He nuzzled his face between her breasts. She thought he was going to pull her shorts down, but he didn't. He stopped.

"Okay, more of that later," he said with a grin and winked. Then he threw on a fresh T-shirt.

They went downstairs. The dark wood parquet flooring gleamed. The couple who ran the B&B waved at them, sitting with their extended family on their tassel-upholstered furniture. It felt like some nobleman's house, with Persian rugs and wall-to-wall bookcases full of ancient-looking books. A soccer game blared from the TV near the fireplace. Leslie noticed a gray cat outside like the one she'd seen on the balcony. Mark took her hand and they walked across to a bar on the plaza.

Mark ordered a beer and she got a glass of wine. They watched the bartender, mesmerized by her long dark braids and tank top. She laughed and smashed the panini sandwiches on the small stove behind her. The place was only big enough to stand and order at the bar. All three stools were occupied by locals watching the soccer game on TV. The bartender shooed Mark and Leslie outside to the tables with umbrellas, where she split open a bag of potato chips into a large glass goblet. Leslie saw the bartender's bicep tattooed with a heart on a fish in an oyster shell.

"*Bene,*" said Leslie.

The girl gave her a raised eyebrow. "*Inglese?*"

"American," said Mark. He scooted his chair closer to the table, grabbed some chips, and took three big gulps of beer.

"*Minuto.* Okay?" said the girl.

"As long as you want," said Mark, wiping his mouth. He winked at the girl.

"*Sì, bene,*" said Leslie to the girl as she walked away.

"This is awful," said Mark, looking into the beer can.

"I think their thing is wine," said Leslie.

He went back in and came out with another beer and their sandwiches.

Leslie took a bite of hot ham, melting cheese, and butter. "Heaven." She shut her eyes and slurped the entire tomato slice.

"Yep, good." When they were done, Mark took their empty plates back. Neon lights blinked on and bugs turned into drops of silver.

"Ready for the city?" She opened her arms wide.

"Let's wait until tomorrow," he sighed, finishing another beer. "I kind of want to fuck my wife before I fall asleep." He crushed the can with his hand.

"Okay, okay," Leslie laughed. The wine and heat and sleepiness made her lean into him.

"You're my wife." He pulled her up, put his lips to her ear. "Hey." He pointed to a convenience store on the corner. "I'll get us some ice cream." They crossed the plaza. "I'll be right back."

A black cat with a white throat dropped from the roof of the convenience store and licked its paw in front of Leslie. None of the cats had collars or tags. She tried to pet the cat, but it disappeared once Mark rattled the door open. They walked back to the B&B unable to eat the cones fast enough, and drips of vanilla trailed on the pavement. Leslie giggled. Mark rubbed his hand up under her shirt. She saw the sea wall that ran behind the B&B in the streetlight. She licked her fingers, but that just made them stickier.

"One look at the ocean?" she said.

"Sure." He lifted Leslie up so she could stand on the sea wall.

The water lapped up to the shore. At intervals, breakwaters of white rocks like lines of teeth divided the sections of the beach. The waves were small, breaking on the shore, making a soft slurry sound. The moon was full.

Mark shrugged. *Why can't he say something sweet?* she wondered.

Back in the room, she waited in bed naked. Mark sat in his striped boxer shorts in the desk chair, scrolling through his phone to look for the vaporetto schedule for the morning. It was midnight.

"Come to bed," she whispered.

"In a sec," he said.

"What happened to my horny husband?" she whispered again, smiling.

"Sorry. Moment passed." He frowned.

Leslie drifted off but woke with a start. Had she heard a door shut? She stretched out her right leg to feel Mark's sleeping body, but he wasn't there. She ran her hand up and down the sheet on his side. It felt cool. She raised herself up. The streetlight helped her see the shapes in the room, the chair on one side, the desk with the towels. The bathroom was dark. A breeze lifted the curtains. A shadow moved outside, and she hopped out of bed.

It was just the gray cat sitting on the ledge of the balcony wall. The one with a small triangle cut out of its ear.

Her eyes got used to the darkness. She went to the desk. His wallet was gone, along with his passport, his phone, his shoes, and the key to the front door of the B&B. He'd gone out, but where? She called him. It was 2 a.m. Nothing. She typed a text: "Just woke up – where are you – can you let me know you are OK?" No reply. She opened the bottom desk drawer where she'd put her travel purse with her passport and an emergency 100-euro note. Everything was there. The black leather cat mask was still there. She threw it on the bed. She wasn't going back to sleep. She threw on her black shorts and a black AC/DC T-shirt, then stuffed her passport and the euro note in one back pocket and her phone in the other.

Clearly, she should be going after her husband, her barely married husband. Crap, they were barely married, and he was gone. He probably couldn't sleep and went for a walk. It was still hot, and all they had was the ceiling fan still whirring at high speed and the bare breeze coming in from the balcony. She looked at the mask on the bed. She'd read that article about people putting on masks in the thirteenth century so they could do things they'd never do otherwise. She grabbed the mask off the bed and stretched the band over her head. He'd laughed at her that she'd never be some hot S&M chick. She pulled the mask down and glanced in the bathroom mirror. *We'll see.* She looked pretty natural.

She flicked her head when the glimmer of her wedding ring stones caught her attention. She rolled her shoulders back and stepped onto the balcony. The cat with the funny ear stared at her and squinted its yellow eyes. The leather against Leslie's skin felt almost cool, and the tension in her forehead relaxed. She started to forget about Mark, about why she was out here with some crazy woman's mask on. She tugged at the edge of the mask that rested on the apple of her cheek, then tried to wedge her fingernail under it. It wouldn't budge. Had it fit *that* snug a minute ago? She felt for the elastic band at the back. Her hair had knotted around it, and the more she tried to free it, the more her hair matted and the band pinched. Once she let it go, she felt fine. Her face under the mask wasn't even sweating. She checked her phone.

Without thinking, she got her sandals and ran out to the balcony. A privacy wall to the right ran straight to the roof, but the divider wall between the balcony and the next unit was stepped. She peeked over. She realized she was estimating how to get herself down there. No one was around. She could walk on the divider wall. She left the sandals and jumped, hardly needing her hands to steady herself. Up on the wall she saw the rows of rooftops leading toward the water and Venice blinking on the horizon. She leaped down to the overhang above the entry door. The night air kept her balanced. Now, she could crawl on one of the two cross beams where a vine of jasmine shot through. By the time one foot felt the beam, the vertical drop didn't matter, and she landed on the sidewalk, all her bones and muscles like liquid.

The rush of adrenaline meant there was no weight to her body. Instead of slapping her feet on the cement, her movements were quick and silent. Three cats loafed at a bench in front of the fountain in the plaza. Maybe Mark had gone to the convenience store? When she got there the lights were on, but the doors had a chain wrapped through the door handles, and the chain was padlocked. The bar where they'd eaten dinner was dark. "Mark." She tried to call his name, but the word felt like it got swallowed in her throat. Out of nowhere she heard the clacking of a skateboard wheels on wood and voices. *There must be a ramp. That's it.* Mark was watching kids skate somewhere. Maybe even skating himself.

She padded west through a park with trees and grass to two wooden ramps and two skaters taking turns. She looked at her phone. Nothing. She watched the boys trick around. She could see perfectly. No Mark. Two cats darted in front of her and she followed them. At the next street she realized she was already at the end of the island, at an inlet that curved into a little dock with small speedboats that she could see below from the railing. At the very end was a wooden boat, older, not sleek or polished. Could Mark have caught the vaporetto to Venice? She opened her phone to find the schedule. They didn't start running again until 6 a.m.

She ran under a blinking yellow traffic light back toward the B&B. It took her no time to make it to the plaza, where several cats lounged, some licking their paws, some curled up. She stopped to check her phone again. Nothing. Maybe he was at the beach? That was it. That's where he was. Waiting for the sun to come up. She ran around to the sea wall. The streetlamp buzzed. One cat wandered past her and jumped up on the wall. It was the gray one with the funny ear. The gray cat stopped, saw something moving. Leslie saw it too. People. A couple. A seagull cawed and flew over them.

The couple was one breakwater over. Leslie climbed down from rock to rock. She could see directly across. She stared. The man had his pants around his feet and was heaving himself into a woman leaning against the rocks opposite. It was Mark. Leslie blinked. She couldn't stop watching Mark's striped boxer shorts. The bartender with the long braids. The muscles in Mark's pale back moved, his body jerked and flexed. The bartender groaned words in Italian. The gray cat flicked its head. Leslie felt her body seize, a cold that was hot paralyzing her, her mouth open, her tongue out. She was crying and nothing could come out. She wanted to die; she hunched down slowly. Then she was at Mark's back, scratching, puncturing, and he was spinning, yelling. The bartender shrieked. Leslie smelled Mark's blood. Her head dropped back and a yowl echoed out of her.

"What the fuck?" Mark yelled, stumbling. Then he stood and looked right through her. "The fuck?" He was holding his hand at his neck, where blood dripped. "What the hell was that?"

The bartender scrambled behind him, pulling her tank top down over her breasts.

The hair on the back of Leslie's neck tingled. She climbed up in two jumps to meet the gray cat on the sea wall. The woman started talking to Mark, who tried to put his pants on. Leslie stayed one more second, panting. Mark's pale body looked like the belly of a dead fish in the night with streaks of dark blood from her scratches. She couldn't look anymore. She ran along the sea wall and pounced onto the street.

The gray cat ran ahead. Leslie turned around to see the sun rising, streaks of yellow, pink, and a line of green. Then she took off. There was something sweet and satisfying about not wanting to look back. She moved the way her body wanted to, her feet barely touching the ground, her momentum increasing, her speed soundless. Her head throbbed. She heard a boat motor throttle. She stopped. It was coming from the little dock. Maybe she could hitch a ride. She raced to the dock, jumped the railing, and headed down the ramp. The old wooden boat she'd seen earlier was idling. The water roiled under its motor.

A woman with long, gray hair pulled the leash lines. If the boat stayed in place, Leslie might make it on board. The woman wore denim overalls. She hunched over the steering column and revved the engine. Leslie darted over the railing as the boat pulled away, fled down the dock, and leaped up, her shadow over the water. She felt her feet skim the bench seat, but she made it over the windshield and dropped on the prow. She should be gasping for air. But she wasn't.

"*Gatto,*" the woman called to her, waving and smiling.

Leslie nodded back. The boat paced at a gentle rhythm through the water. Leslie leaned over and saw her reflection in the glossy dark of the Adriatic. The cat mask was still attached, but now she could wedge her index finger under it. She pushed the mask up on her forehead and looked back at the woman driving the boat. The woman's eyes were slits and her left ear was cut.

"I'm leaving my husband." Leslie waved her arm.

"*Sì, Signora,*" said the woman.

Leslie felt her wedding ring, pulled it off, and lobbed it into the Adriatic.

"Hotel Danieli?" Leslie yelled to the woman above the noise

of the motor. She felt in her back pocket for her passport, took out the euro note, and handed it to the woman.

"*Sì, bene,*" said the woman, smiling. She pointed ahead.

Leslie faced the entrance to the Grand Canal. Her body felt calm. She yawned and stretched. She leaned back on her elbows and looked down at her bare feet as Venice opened for her. The buildings reared up, tall, tiered, fragile fortresses reflecting on the water's surface. She would stay in the honeymoon suite. She would eat bowl after bowl of gelato. She pulled the mask down just enough to shade her eyes and wondered who had left it behind.

12

THE ENCOUNTER - CORNELIA FEYE

Arm in arm, the couple walked down the crowded lane in Madrid's old city center. The sun hung low and shadows stretched long on the cobblestones. Families, lovers, and groups of teenagers in skinny jeans were out in the hours after siesta and before dinner. Time for tapas and beer. Time to roam the streets in search of a restaurant, a friend, an evening entertainment, or simply a stroll.

The woman was giddy with excitement to be in Europe, to be part of this crowd, anticipating the pleasant evening that lay ahead like a wrapped present. What would it bring? What would they find? What delicacies lay ahead? What heady wines?

The man and the woman entered a small tapas bar on the Plaza de Santa Ana. The bar had been there since 1917. They marveled at the intricate tiles; the old mahogany counter, polished by generations of elbows leaning on it; the black-and-white photos of bullfights and Spanish pride. They ordered *vino rojo*, grilled *pulpo*, and a Spanish potato tortilla, delighted by the old-world charm of their surroundings.

～

Antoine observed them through the open window. They looked comfortable with each other, compatible in age; they'd probably been married for many years, judging from their wedding rings.

Antoine thought about his own parents. They would have been this couple's age, if they had lived. But his father had been killed by Boko Haram, his sister kidnapped, his mother raped. Antoine's jaw hardened. His eyes burned black with hate. He was the only survivor of the family, because he had been out when the attack happened. Why couldn't his parents sit here, enjoying a mild evening?

～

After the tapas, the couple walked to a quiet restaurant named Rincón. Several other restaurants along the way had the same name.

"I wonder if Rincón is the name of a popular Madrid family," the husband remarked.

"*Rincón* just means 'corner,'" the woman answered.

A man brushed by her, in a hurry. For a moment she saw his sharp profile: a pinched dark face, sharp cheekbones, hair long and unruly, eyes darting, deep black, haunted. He rushed in front of her and disappeared into the crowd, diving into a shop. Why was he in such a rush? This was happy hour, the time between day and night.

～

Antoine followed the blond woman. She was new in town, from Germany or the United States, from the look of her. He dreamt about both countries, wanted to go there more than anything, but they were unattainable. Coming to Spain, making it this far, had been hard enough.

Why did she have to flaunt her happiness and good fortune? Laughing, smiling, with stars in her eyes, on the arm of her man, who looked distinguished, successful, self-confident. The man smiled back at the woman, indulgently, happy to share this moment, but also aware, on guard. For a split second their gazes met. The man's eyes narrowed suspiciously. Of course he didn't trust Antoine. He was African and the man was white, middle-aged, used to getting his way.

Of course the man would immediately assume that Antoine was up to no good, poor, a migrant, because of the color of his skin and his shabby dress. And the man was right. Antoine was a migrant. On his way from Gabon through Libya across the Mediterranean to Spain, he had seen horrors this couple could never even imagine. Eight months of living hell. He had seen fellow travelers drown, had been held captive in a Libyan prison that was too crude even for animals. He had walked for miles in rain, heat, mud, and freezing cold. He had been held in a makeshift camp in Lampedusa, without toilets, water, or proper shelter. But he had pressed on; he'd never given up when others were sent back to sub-Saharan Africa. He was determined to reach Europe and the fabulous riches and lifestyle he had seen on television shows in his homeland, and dreamt about. Only to arrive and watch his dream evaporate. He was shut out. There were no jobs here for him. He had no papers. He spoke the wrong language. Had the wrong skin color. Was unwanted.

This couple paraded in front of him, giddy with happiness and good fortune forever out of his reach. How he hated them. Why did they have so much and he so little? They did not deserve it. He had suffered so deeply to get here. And for what?

∽

The walls of the restaurant were covered with photographs of the owner, Esteban, accompanied by various other people. The couple looked for familiar faces of celebrities and asked the dignified waiter about them.

"These are all important customers," he explained.

"Any famous people?" the woman wanted to know.

"Some politicians," the waiter said evasively.

The couple smiled. Obviously the owner liked his own image, despite his balding head and chubby stature. They ordered the house specialties, rabbit stew and bean soup. As they toasted and raised their glasses filled with the deep red wine of the region, the woman said, "I feel so fortunate. I don't know if I deserve all this."

"You deserve so much more than this," the man said.

After dinner, she offered to pay and fumbled for the purse she had deposited on the back of her chair. Normally she wore it with the strap across her chest, close to her body. She remembered jamming her phone, her wallet, and her lipstick into the small pouch before they left the hotel. It barely fit. Now the purse felt light in her hands.

She opened it with a sinking feeling.

"Oh God, my wallet is gone," she moaned.

The blood drained from her head, which felt suddenly unattached to her body. Slightly buzzed from the wine, the woman felt the velvety night dissolving. The pleasant feeling of floating on air snapped and deposited her on the harsh cobblestone ground of reality.

"You must have left it in the hotel," the man said, and he paid with his credit card.

"I don't think so," she stammered, but they rushed down the narrow lane. The charming sounds from the bars and taverns now sounded hollow and deceptive.

When they arrived in their hotel room, she confirmed the wallet was gone.

"You were careless—you always leave your purse open," he scolded.

"I tried to be careful," she wailed. "I carried it close to me. How could anybody have reached into that tiny purse and taken my wallet without me noticing?"

"You don't pay attention. I think I know what happened."

"I think I do too." She hung her head.

"The man with the empty eyes who bumped into you," he said accusingly.

"I am sorry. I feel so stupid."

They retraced their steps to the tapas bar where they had started the evening. No wallet there. The streets now felt threatening. Within seconds, everything had changed.

"I told you over and over to be careful." He sounded angry, annoyed, disappointed.

"I already feel bad enough. Please don't yell at me."

"We have to call the credit card companies now."

They rushed back to their hotel and spent the next two hours on the phone, arguing and cancelling cards.

∼

Antoine ran into a sneaker store, triumphant. He had snagged the woman's wallet from her purse when he bumped into her. For a moment he thought the man would notice, but the crowd around them was thick and he had darted quickly through the throng of people into the shop. In a corner, shielded by customers, he looked inside the wallet: two hundred dollars. He'd been right. They were Americans. About 120 euros, two credit cards. The cards were probably useless. He wouldn't be able to use them before the couple cancelled them, and they could lead to his capture. After all, he didn't look like a woman with a European name. The money was not a great amount, but enough to buy new sneakers, and a twelve-pack of beer and a pizza to take back to the room he shared with four other refugees on the outskirts of Madrid. He'd put money toward rent and set aside $50 to send to his extended family back in Gabon. He couldn't tell them how he'd gotten the money. They thought he was working, making a living in Spain, earning money to pay back the savings his entire family had collected for the smuggler to take him to Europe. He could never tell them the truth. All their hopes rested on him.

∼

The woman lay in her hotel bed in the dark, listening to the even breathing of her husband beside her. She couldn't sleep.

The missing wallet burned a hole into her mind. How could she have been so stupid and naïve? It was only her second evening here. How could she manage to spend the rest of her time here? She had been too self-absorbed to realize that there were many desperate people out there, ready to resort to desperate measures.

Hours ticked by as she tossed and turned. How long was her husband going to be angry with her? How long was she going to be mad at herself? She had to make peace with the situation.

From outside, the noises of the night floated through the open window. The clinking of cutlery, the scraping of chairs, the closing bang of shutters, the bark of a dog.

It wasn't the city's fault. It wasn't my fault—well, maybe a little— it wasn't even the thief's fault, the woman thought.

We all just came together in this place, at this time. Through this constellation of circumstances a situation arose. There was a need, desperation, and abundance. One took from the other. That's how the universe works. Surplus flows to fill the void. One was the tool, the victim, the other was the winner, who gained from the encounter.

Maybe something good will come of it, the woman thought. *Maybe it will help in a small way. I will stop feeling like a victim, and will make this donation willingly. Hopefully it will not just go toward buying drugs. If I submit this amount consciously, then the shame and the feeling of violation will disappear.*

She looked at the sleeping man beside her. Corrective action had been taken. Nobody had been hurt. He was already over it. So was she. She closed her eyes, and the thoughts and emotions evaporated into velvety spaciousness. She finally fell asleep.

13

MISS SEGOVIA - JENNIFER M. FRANKS

Calle de Arlabán No. 10, Madrid, Spain, 1912

Señor Manuel Ramírez scraped a chisel along a thin cedar plank with quick, precise movements. Paper-thin shavings of wood curled ahead of his instrument. He blew them away and inspected the grain, his keen eyes looking for imperfections. On the walls around his shop hung saws, hammers, gouges, picks, and sanding devices. On a far table sat unfinished guitars bound with twine while the glue dried, adhering their pieces together. The scent of rosewood, cedar, and spruce hung in the air. Sr. Ramírez ran a finger along the plank. He would make a fine guitar from this aged piece of wood and a skilled player would bring it to life, cherishing its rich tones.

The bells on the front door jingled, calling his attention. Sr. Ramírez put down the chisel and clapped the dust from his hands. He had to sell guitars to stay in business. He left his workshop to see who had come into his store.

A ridiculous-looking youth stood in the gallery, staring at the guitars on display. He wore striped trousers, a black velvet waistcoat with silver buttons, a wide-brimmed black hat, a billowing scarf, and black leather shoes with oversized buckles, and he carried a walking stick. Sr. Ramírez nearly burst into laughter at the sight of him. He looked like a child in a clown suit. Coughing away a chuckle into his hand, Sr. Ramírez greeted him. "How may I help you, sir?"

The boy's dark eyes gleamed through the round, black-rimmed glasses perched on his sharp nose. "I should like some assistance."

"Well, I shall see to it that you are treated with the diligence and care you deserve." Sr. Ramírez smiled with amusement.

The boy squinted back at him suspiciously. He stood taller and feigned a commanding tone, announcing, "I'm here to rent your finest guitar."

"We don't rent guitars. We only sell them."

"I can't afford one," he replied flatly. If Sr. Ramírez hadn't found him so entertaining, he would have rushed him out of his shop at once. "I am Señor Ramírez and this is my store. What is your name?"

"I'm Andrés Segovia. I am a guitarist and some friends from Córdoba recommended me to you, sir." He extended a hand. "They say you are the best luthier in town."

Sr. Ramírez shook the boy's hand. "Ah, Segovia. The echoes of your name have reached this house. It seems the whole of Sevilla took to the streets last year to listen to you," he teased.

The boy's face reddened. "That wasn't well attended, I know," he admitted sheepishly, "but I arrived in Madrid a few days ago and I intend to give an audition in the Ateneo soon. Señor Ramírez, the guitar I have does not satisfy my requirements. I would like you to allow me to use your best guitar."

Sr. Ramírez frowned; the request was absurd.

The boy pressed further. "It goes without saying that I believe it reasonable that you should stipulate a fair allowance for this lease, the way a piano shop rents pianos. And I am willing, if you like, to pay in advance. Furthermore, if the guitar is completely to my liking, I will ask you to sell it to me."

Sr. Ramírez was confounded. He had never thought of

renting his guitars to traveling players, let alone one of his finest pieces.

"I should be able to purchase it soon anyway," the boy added quickly, "if the illusions I bring to Madrid do not turn to disenchantment when I touch the crude reality."

Sr. Ramírez had to laugh. It was a *crude reality* when a guitarist had no audience. Still, he couldn't possibly loan his finest guitar to him. It was too risky. Who's to say he wouldn't disappear with it? Only a fool would do such a thing. And who's to say the boy could even play?

"Well, what do you say, Señor Ramirez?"

Sr. Ramírez thought for a moment. The boy had to have some skill if the Ateneo hired him, didn't he? It was the biggest venue in town for music, art, and science exhibitions, but he couldn't draw a crowd in Sevilla, where they lie in wait for a good player . . . and his attire and manner of speaking were ridiculous. Chances were, he was all show, with marginal talent at best.

"Please, Señor," the boy pleaded.

"Nobody has ever asked me for such a thing." *I should just kick this kid out and get back to work,* Sr. Ramírez thought, *I can't waste my time on someone who can't afford to buy. But . . . then again, maybe this kid makes sense. If pianos are rented for concerts, why not guitars?* He finally made up his mind. "I'll have to hear you play first."

"I'd love to!" the boy replied brightly.

"Follow me."

Andrés followed Sr. Ramírez through swinging doors to the workshop in the rear of the store.

"Santos!" Sr. Ramírez called out. "Bring me my finest guitar."

Santos, an assistant luthier, appeared, giving his boss a questioning look. "Go ahead, hand it over to him," Sr. Ramírez said. Reluctantly, Santos handed Andrés the highly valuable guitar. Andrés inspected it with an expression of wonder. Turning it over in his hands, he ran his fingers along the smooth, hourglass curves of its cherry-stained body. It smelled like a humidor, where choice cigars aged until the bitterness left their leaves.

"The back is made of Brazilian rosewood, the top is spruce," Sr. Ramírez said with obvious pride.

"It's absolutely beautiful!" Andrés replied, noticing the delicate rosette pattern around the sound hole. Some of the tuning peg holes had been filled in with wood, showing the instrument had once been an eleven-string guitar, but was now the standard six-string.

The bell on the door jingled again and Sr. José Hierro, a violin professor from the Conservatorio Superior, joined them in the workshop.

"You've come just in time, Professor," Sr. Ramírez said. "This young man is about to play for us. He's giving a concert at the Ateneo." Professor Hierro nodded but looked skeptical. He'd seen many an audition fall short of his expectations.

"May I play now?" Andrés asked, anxious to play the fine instrument.

"Yes, of course, please." Sr. Ramírez motioned him to a nearby stool.

Andrés sat and placed his fingers on the fretboard. He closed his eyes and remained motionless for some time. Santos gave Sr. Ramírez a doubtful look, but he responded with a raised hand, asking for patience. The fact that the boy took his time to mentally prepare was promising.

An explosion of sound rang out when the boy's fingers began to move along the neck of the guitar. His youthful expression was replaced by a mask of intense fury. Sr. Ramírez's heart began to race as he watched the boy's sudden transformation and realized what he was playing. It was Bach. Nobody had ever adapted a Bach cello suite for the guitar before. It was too complicated, too difficult . . . too impossible. Yet, this boy was doing so with an aggressive technique that was emotional, powerful, and stirring. Santos gaped when Andrés transitioned from forceful strumming to feather-soft tremolos in a display of skill beyond his years.

Andrés finished the score, out of breath. "Señor Ramírez, this is truly the most beautiful guitar I've ever played!"

The three men, astounded by what they had just witnessed, simply stared. Professor Hierro spoke first. "Bravo, young man! I like your temperament and your technical ease. It's a pity these qualities are fruitless on the guitar. Are you going to banish the talent with which God has gifted you? Do you want to switch instruments? The guitar is beautiful, but lonely and uncultured. You are still young. The violin will make you famous."

Andrés smiled wanly. "Thank you, Professor, but I fear it may be too late to switch to another instrument. Besides, I can assure you that I could not betray my guitar. She needs me. The violin doesn't."

Professor Hierro raised his brows. "Very well, young man."

"My boy," Sr. Ramírez said, "that was absolutely masterful. If you promise me you will continue to play . . . the guitar is yours."

"Really?" Andrés was incredulous. "Not to rent?"

"Not to rent. Yours to keep as a gift from me to you."

The boy lit up with a triumphant smile. "I promise I will play, and with this instrument, always."

"Take it with you around the world. That will be my payment."

∼

Munich, Germany, 1924

Hermann Hauser, a German luthier in his early forties, took his center seat in the first row of the music hall. He immediately fixed his eyes upon the Spanish guitar on stage, propped up on a stand beside an empty chair. A garish spotlight shined upon it. Laughter and conversation levels rose in the chambers of the hall as it filled with people, but Hauser didn't notice. He could see striations in the wood on the body of the guitar, and places of wear on the fretboard. There were no scratches beneath the sound hole, where an overzealous strum would have left its mark. This guitar had never suffered such an insult, nor had it ever produced an errant sound. This guitar was cherished, and never played with amplification that would alter its pitch.

The lights dimmed and a rumble of applause replaced the chatter. Hauser stood to clap as Andrés Segovia, in a dark suit and thick, round glasses strode onto the stage, waving his hand. Without pretense, Segovia sat, placed his left foot on a low pedestal, and reached for his Ramírez guitar. He positioned it across his lap and immediately tuned the pegs. Without a word, he began to play a soothing melody. His expression relaxed to a gentle calm that carried from one song into the next. Hauser marveled at his effortless manner, his agile fingers, his total mastery of the instrument. The Ramírez guitar had such clear, mellow, balanced tones. Hauser couldn't wait to measure it, weigh it, study its inner skeleton, inspect how it was constructed and figure out how it projected such perfect sound.

After the concert, an anxious Hauser held a paper that stated he was allowed to meet with Segovia. The guards let him through. When he entered the hotel suite, he found Segovia resting in a chair, sipping a glass of sherry. Segovia rose to greet his guest.

"Hello, I'm Hermann Hauser." He held Segovia's dark, gentle eyes, enlarged through the thick lenses of his black, square frames.

"Ah yes, you're the luthier that requested to inspect my guitar," Segovia replied, shaking his hand.

"It would be an honor to do so, Maestro. Thank you for accepting my request."

"I couldn't pass up your challenge. Please, she's all yours. Take as much time as you need."

Hauser saw the guitar on the table and immediately went to work. He jotted down numbers, notes, and measurements in a journal, even writing down the placement of sweat drops that had permanently stained the wood. "You call it a *she*?" he commented.

"Yes. A guitar has feminine curves, and this influences her behavior. Sometimes it is impossible to deal with her, but most of the time she is very sweet. If you caress her properly, she will sing beautifully. I call her *Miss Segovia*."

Hauser chuckled. "Do you play her eight hours a day?"

"Longer hours are useless. Artists who says they play eight hours or more every day are either liars or asses." Hauser burst into laughter as he continued taking measurements. Although soft-spoken, he found Segovia witty and honest.

"You say your father was a luthier as well?" Segovia asked.

"Yes, Josef Hauser. He taught me everything I know. Mainly, how to build zithers and lutes, but guitars are my instruments of choice."

"Mine too, and only my Ramírez. I have played no other since the day she was gifted to me by Señor Ramírez himself."

"I could hear why; *she* is flawless."

"And you think you can build me a guitar to compete with my affection for *her*?"

"That is the challenge, sir, yes," admitted Hauser. "Give me one year to build my finest Hauser guitar, using these same specifications, and see if I can win your favor."

Segovia laughed lightheartedly. "I can't make any promises. I adore my Ramírez, but in one year's time, you may present to me your best effort."

"That is all I ask. I thank you for the opportunity, Maestro Segovia. I'll see you next year with a *Hauser* guitar."

～

Hermann Hauser sorted through stacks of spruce until he selected two perfect planks. He planed them to a smooth finish, glued their thin edges together, then clamped them securely in place to dry. The next day, he measured and drew the hourglass shape of a guitar onto the plank, sawed it free, and sanded it smooth. He cut out a sound hole and chiseled a circular groove around its perimeter to embed a decorative rosette. The following day, he chose a piece of Indian rosewood to make a guitar neck. He added an ebony fretboard and cut nineteen grooves to hammer in the fret wires. He glued on a peghead, where he would later hollow out six holes to insert tuning pegs. He selected, cut, planed, sanded, chiseled, and glued an inner skeleton to the guitar's body.

He made slow progress each day by skillfully adding another element to the body of the guitar. After ten months, it was ready for staining, and he finally painted on a layer of lacquer. He added the bridge, metal hardware on the peghead, and eventually pulled nylon strings taut by twisting the tuning pegs. He let the guitar rest, knowing the strain the strings put upon the newly built frame. After some time, he tuned the guitar and strummed it gently. A beautiful, clear sound emanated. Hauser smiled to himself. This was the one. He made travel arrangements by train to Switzerland, where Segovia was residing.

~

"Hello, Hermann! How have you been?" Segovia asked.

"Faring well, and you?" Hauser placed the guitar case on the table.

"No complaints; a full house at every performance. Is this the one?"

Hauser opened the case to reveal a polished guitar.

"Beautiful," Segovia murmured. "May I?"

"Absolutely." Hauser watched him lift the guitar from the case, making note of his expression while he inspected it. He looked pleased.

Segovia took a seat and placed the guitar over his crossed knees. The long fingernails of his right hand began to pluck strings, while his left hand rattled through scale patterns. Segovia strummed all six of the strings. He stopped playing abruptly and handed the guitar back to Hauser. "It is a beautiful guitar, a faithful replica, but I will not play it."

Hauser winced. "May I ask why not?"

Segovia shook his head sadly. "It has no soul."

Hauser nodded with humility. It was disappointing news,

but he would not be discouraged. "Very well, Maestro, I will build you a better one. I'll see you next year?"

"I don't know where I'll be . . . Italy, France, maybe Austria . . ."

"Don't worry, you're easy to find."

～

Segovia rejected Hauser's guitar the following year, and two the year after that. "Not enough volume," he said. Upon every return to his workshop, Hauser scratched his head and went back to his sketches. He made innovative tweaks to his design and chose different woods to save on weight, add strength, and improve sound.

By the fifth year, Hauser accepted Segovia's rejection rather quickly, and they had lunch together, chatting about their families and the upcoming holidays. Segovia made some helpful suggestions and Hauser jotted down more notes, anxious to implement the new changes in his next design.

In year ten, the Hauser guitar was once again rejected, and year eleven had the same disappointing outcome. Hauser and Segovia talked of music and politics, and sipped wine. "Will you try again?" Segovia asked. They were sharing a cigar on the patio of Segovia's home overlooking the Andalusian countryside.

"I will not abandon the challenge I set forth for myself."

"You've made some marvelous instruments over the years, and each one an improvement over the last."

"Marvelous, but not enough to replace *Miss Segovia*."

"No. But, I like your drive, Hermann. A lesser man would have quit long ago."

"Your rejections have only served to motivate me."

Segovia nodded his agreement, raising his wineglass. "Best of luck, my friend."

"Until next year."

◌

Hermann Hauser took twice the normal time to select the aged spruce, rosewood, mahogany, bone, and ebony he would use on his next guitar. He omitted cedar. He revisited his father's notes, as well as those from the famous nineteenth-century Spanish luthier Antonio de Torres. Hauser worked tirelessly for months on the latest guitar in his workshop. Then, as he had done for the last twelve years, he placed the finished guitar in a case and departed to find Segovia.

Segovia greeted Hauser with a firm embrace. He opened and lifted a pale, rather plain guitar from its case and sat in a chair. "Let's see what you've made this year, my friend." He began to play and almost immediately cocked his head to the side, listening closely. His eyes narrowed as he plucked individual strings and played natural harmonics on the seventh and twelfth frets. Hauser had never seen him react this way, and he held his breath. Segovia played a song with great intensity, then abruptly stopped. Looking up, he said, "Hermann, this is the greatest guitar of our epoch."

Hermann Hauser threw his hands up in the air and clenched them into tight, triumphant fists.

◌

Andrés Segovia set aside his Manuel Ramírez guitar and played only his Hermann Hauser. Segovia is credited with bringing the Spanish classical guitar, once a mere parlor instrument, to the world stage. His career spanned seven decades. In 1962, while Segovia was in the recording studio, a microphone fell into his Hauser guitar and it never sounded the same to him again. Both of Segovia's Ramírez and Hauser guitars are currently on display in the Metropolitan Museum of Art in New York City.

14

DIRTY WINDOWS - TABATHA TOVAR

I f my arms weren't so heavy and the day so hot, I'd totally get up. I'm supposed to get the mail, but the driveway will make me all dusty and I still have to go to the antique shop and help Mom. It's not fair. Dan should work a longer shift. Why am I expected to be patient and help her when even my big brother gets frustrated and has short shifts? I mean, she fine by herself. At least for a little while. I'll count out the register later, but she's got her notebooks so she remembers the things she's supposed to remember. Besides, who makes a thirteen-year-old walk outside on days like this and go to work? Child labor laws, anyone? It's 1983, not 1883. There are rules now. And why is it so hot? At least the floor is cool. It's the only place cool enough to bear in this house.

At least I can look out my window from down here on the floor next to my bed. Well, sort of. I can barely see the sky for all the dirt on the glass. I remember when no weekend was complete without me on a chair outside the house wiping down the windows with vinegar. Mom stood inside until the chicken farm next door became visible. "You can stop," she'd say, "when I can count the freckles on your nose." And only then. Afterwards, I'd hide in the coolness of our shop's storeroom and play with paper dolls from books too damaged to sell in the store.

But that was "BC," as my brother Dan and I call it. "Before Car Crash." Before Crazy. Before my eight-year-old self learned phrases like "traumatic brain injury" and "activities of daily living." Before cranky and yelling and forgetting. Before the woman I knew changed into the woman I know. The woman who finds it hard enough to just go to work. She carries notebooks of schedules and reminders and suggestions, and nowhere did she write that the windows need to be clean. So they're not. I suppose it's the only benefit of the new, less improved Mom. These days, the windows are only good for judging when day has turned to night as light tan turns to black. I miss BC Mom, sometimes. BC Mom made us do chores, but also made cookies and told funny stories and took us into the city to go to the zoo and ride on the trolley. BC Mom didn't sleep all the time and have headaches and say sorry so much that it doesn't mean anything anymore. BC Mom didn't look at us with tears because she remembers so much from long ago and so little from right now. BC. I'd wash the windows if I could get BC Mom back.

I roll my arm from over my head to under the bed and grab my suitcase of paper dolls. I love this suitcase. I love all of the old suitcases and trunks and doctor bags at the shop. I like to know where they're from and when they were made. I know everything about all the pieces that come into our shop. Every time we get something new, I draw a quick picture of it and write out its name, price, and any history I know about on a little card to be displayed next to it. About half the store is now consignment, so I get to hear each piece's story from a personal perspective. I write it all down. This way Mom doesn't have to remember and can just ring it up on the register and I can take it out of inventory later. It's our system. With Mom, everything is a system, and one that never changes.

This old travel bag is special because I saved it. We were trying to sell it on consignment, but the leather was all scuffed and two of the brass purse feet were gone, leaving holes in the bottom. No one bought it. When the owners came to take home the things that didn't sell, they wanted to throw it out, so I asked if I could have it. They gave it to me. Its warm brown leather is still so beautiful. It traveled all over the world since the 1920s, and someday I'll take it with me around the world again. I don't care that the leather straps are missing and the lining is all ripped. I imagine it as it was, and someday I'll fix things like this back up and make them like new. When Dan and I grow up we can run the shop. I'll restore stuff in back and Dan can deal with customers in front. I rub my fingers over the remnants of once beautiful brass clasps. Old things are beautiful. Families saved them and took care of them and passed them on from parent to child because families didn't run away from each other. They stayed together. The way they are supposed to.

My paper dolls live in this travel case. Dan teases me about the dolls. Of course he does. Boys are annoying. But still, on my birthday, he gets me another one. I sit up to lift the lid and look at the twelve ladies lying face up on a pile of beautiful paper dresses. Each dress is a drawing of the elegant style of its time with a lace bodice, cinched waist, and fashionably modest long sleeves.

If I'd been born when these dresses were in fashion, I'd wear the same kinds of flowing skirts with satin and lace boots that had little pewter buttons. Father would live with us and Mother would make us all promenade after an early supper. Maybe I'd have an accent—a New York accent or maybe British. I could be a princess and my brother a prince. We'd live in a castle—where the ceilings are so high that no one would call me freakishly tall. Everything would be easy if we were born then. I'd have servants and gentleman callers and a nanny who always smiled and always took care of me.

I pull out my three favorite dolls, beautiful women with serious expressions, and pinch down the tabs of their paper dresses.

I hear him walk into the house. The screen door slams and he jingles as he takes long steps down the hallway. I imagine him in a prince costume and with bells on his shoes making that noise. But I'm not stupid. I know they're not bells, not really, but a chain that attaches his wallet to his jeans and clinks as he walks. I know he wants to talk, but it's too hot. Maybe we can talk tomorrow. Or the day after that.

I pick up my two prettiest dolls and walk them over the tiles until they face one another. "Hello, darrrrrling," I say in a high-pitched voice. The kind of voice that really rich people on TV use. "Aren't you looking so lovely today." I walk the dark-haired doll over to kiss the cheeks of the blonde. I try to put on a British accent because this other doll is from England. She's royalty. "Why, thank you, Madam. And may I say that you, too, are in top form."

Dan clears his throat. He's tapping something against the door frame. It's annoying. I am not ready to talk to him. "Vic, it's your turn to work. Mom's still at the shop. I gotta go."

He drops something on the floor and I try not to flinch. If I don't turn around, I can pretend it's his backpack. Or maybe a present for me. If I keep my face away from him and stare at the dolls, I can pretend I don't know that it's a suitcase. An ugly one. A new one that is not cherished and passed down through the family but made for running away.

"I know you can hear me, Vic," he says.

"Stop calling me Vic. I'm not a boy." I sit up and look at him. I move my shoulder forward, gracefully. "Vic is a gentleman's name. Refer to me as Victoria." I pick up a doll and run my fingers across her face. She's so pretty. So confident. "I'll go to the shop in a minute. But you, you can't go anywhere. Not today. Put that bag back in your room and finish up your chores."

Dan leaves his suitcase by my door and walks in to sit beside me. He picks up one of my paper ladies, rights her dress, and hands her to me. "Sorry, it's gotta be today. School's starting soon and I gotta get a place. But, you're right. I can do a couple more things before I go. What would you like me to do before I go?" With him next to me I feel my eyes getting all slippery, and I don't like it. When Dad left, Dan took care of me. When we lost

BC Mom, he took care of me. I imagine briefly a home where he is not in it, and a feeling in my stomach comes screaming up my throat and I can't breathe. He can't go. It won't be home without him. If I can keep him busy, well, maybe I won't have to wake up in a house without him in it.

"Tons of things. Like . . ." I look around my room and point to my closet. "Like those boxes. I need to get them down and I can't."

"I can do that."

"And the windows need to be washed." I hold up one of the dolls and say in my rich woman accent again, "How is a lady to see if her gentleman callers are coming if she cannot see through the glass?"

He laughs and walks over to the closet. "Vic—Victoria, I don't believe you'll have 'gentleman callers' anytime soon, and if you call guys that, maybe never."

I lie back, draping my arm over my forehead, and continue to talk in my accent. "And how are we to obtain nourishment? You are leaving us to be perished."

"To perish, not 'to be perished.' And there will be no perishing. You two will be fine. Lots of people help out, you know." He reaches up and easily pulls the boxes off the top shelf. I should have thought of something harder to do. Stupid boxes. Nothing in them but stuffed animals I don't want anymore and artwork from elementary school. He stands up after the second box is on the floor and looks down at me. "I wouldn't leave if I didn't think you guys could handle it. Give me some credit. But Victoria, it's college. It's my time to go." He smiles a stupid I'm-so-smart smile.

I want him to sit down again. I want to crawl in his lap and close my eyes and know that he'll make everything alright. He always does. But if he leaves, who will take care of Mom? Who will make sure she gets to work and the orders get made and that the house doesn't burn down because she forgot a potpie in the oven? If he goes, who will take care of me?

"That it? You ready to go to the shop? Mom's there alone

now." He has his hands pressed into his lower back like an old man. Like Dad did.

Dad. I don't really remember him, but I remember the night he left. I was five and Mom was crying. I found Dan in the front room, staring out the window to the driveway toward the street. There was nothing to see but stars. Stars shot up into the sky like a handful of glowing glitter stuck on the ceiling. I held Dan's hand and he squeezed it hard. "It'll be alright, Vic. I'll take care of you."

But now he's going, too. Who is going to make it alright now? Not Mom.

"If Mom's alone, then you should go help her." I turn back to my dolls. I don't want him seeing me cry.

"No, it's your turn. Besides, my car's gassed up and I want to beat traffic, so . . ."

"So you have a lot more to do. You can't just leave us like this."

Dan rubs his hands through his hair and paces a little. He taps his foot on the ground a few times and leaves my room briefly before coming back with a pen and paper. "Alright." His voice is a little raised. He hands me a pencil and a piece of paper ripped from a notebook. "Write down a couple of things you want me to do before I go and I'll give you an hour. An hour. That's it, though."

I write down as many things as I can think of: cut firewood for the winter, rinse the trash cans, rotate the compost, wash the windows, and make sure Mom's car has air in the tires and the battery is fine and whatever else cars need. He pulls the paper out of my hand while I'm writing the last part.

"Firewood? Really? It's like two hundred degrees. And, you won't need Mom's car. You can't drive—and neither can she."

"Well, I can't really be sure when you're coming back, right? Am I supposed to cut the firewood? And the car, well, we might need help, and if someone else's car is broken they could use hers."

"Fine. I'll start with the firewood. Call someone to stay with

Mom for the next hour and then we'll head up there. Got it, Vic?"

"Victoria."

"Got it, Victoria? One hour."

"Fine." I turn away as he stomps off and jump as the back door slams. I get up and walk next to his suitcase. It's a black hard-shelled case that BC Mom got for a trip she never ended up taking. The sticker from his band is plastered on the side. Now they're going to need a new guitarist. I kick the suitcase right in the middle of the band sticker. It falls over. I thought I could kick it harder than that. I was hoping to kick the ugly thing so hard it'd disappear into Mom's room. Disappear. What if it did disappear? If he couldn't find it, he couldn't leave.

With that thought in mind, I grab the suitcase and shut the front door quietly behind me. I hear the rhythmic sound of Dan hammering a wedge through the bulky logs as I lumber up the driveway toward town, pulled side to side by the case.

~

It's around here somewhere; I just know it. My eyes scan the driveways ahead of me. There it is—a driveway hidden by oleanders.

I slip between branches, pulling the case behind me and listening to cracks as small stems bend and break. I head down the tree-lined driveway toward an empty house. Dan brought me here a couple years ago, telling me it reminded him of *Sleeping Beauty*. "Remember," he said, "how the fairies put everyone to sleep while the princess slept and a forest grew around the castle? This is like that castle."

At first glance, it appears unkempt but not abandoned. I hide the suitcase in the bushes in front of the house and jump the fence in order to walk through the broken back door into the home's emptiness. My arms tremble from holding the case so long and I shake blood back into my fingers. We never told anyone about this place. It was ours. I played with my paper dolls while Dan played guitar. I touch the walls and they feel like they're vibrating. It's as if they still echo with his songs.

I drag my foot through the dust and dirt on the floor, making patterns. I want to be here knowing that he's home waiting. Maybe he'll be mad, but at least he won't be gone. I know that stealing his bag won't keep him home forever, but I'm just trying to get a little time to think of a plan that will help him stay. I know he wants to stay here with us. How could he want to leave us?

As I sneeze, I notice that the front windows get a little lighter. Oh no! He's here? Of course he's here. Jumping behind the front door, I hear tires squeal to a halt and three doors shut in front of the house. I start to run toward the back of the house, but a man's shadow rises on the floor, so I quietly scramble back behind the door and watch the shadow's arms raise like the man is looking inside. Can't be Dan—he's not that big. This is a man, not my brother. But who?

I slide down the door, trying to make myself small. Disappear. A loud pound on the door behind my back startles me and I fall onto the dirty tile. I bring dusty palms over my mouth to keep myself from screaming.

"She's got to be here. Go around back." It *is* Dan. I hear three people thumping over the fence into the backyard.

My heart scrambles into my throat. My feet slide on the slippery tile as I right myself and turn toward the front door. I open the door and can't remember where I hid his suitcase. I have to find it. I have to keep him here. I see it in the bushes and fish it out. By the time I've gotten it and started down the walkway to the street, Dan is standing in the hallway, looking at me. His face is red and I want to cry. I've never seen him this mad before. I don't want him to be mad, I just don't want him to be gone. He steps forward and I run across the dry grass, to the asphalt.

"Hey, come back!" he yells, lifting one hand in the air as if to signal me.

"Leave me alone," is all I can get out. My arms burn. The case feels heavier than it had been and scrapes the ground. I start to run, but the ground shifts below me as if made of sand. My back aches and all I can think is that I need to get away, to hide, so I can have more time.

"Enough, Vic. Victoria. Stop. I found you. Gimme my stuff back." He stops on the porch, leaning forward and resting heavily on his thighs. He's catching his breath or he's getting poised to sprint.

I face him. "No, not unless you promise not to go!" I shout.

He hangs his head and breathes deeply. This is how we fight, how we've always fought. He looks away and I feel bad, and I run and put my arms around him and call him my prince and he smiles. But if I go to him now, I'll lose. He'll win and he'll be gone and I'll be left in this castle alone. No! I can't let him go. I can't just let him leave me.

Dan lifts his head. "Look, Victoria, I have to go. It's college. It's my turn and then it'll be yours." He takes a step forward and I instinctively flinch back. Up the driveway I see where his car had plowed down the oleanders, making the home visible from the road. That's why the front room seemed to get brighter. He let in more light. The square hole at the top of the road looks like a window. Cleaned.

"You don't *have* to. You *want* to. You want to leave me here stuck taking care of Mom." My face tightens. My hands hurt. I squeeze the handle more tightly. I inch myself away toward the light. There's got to be another place to hide up there somewhere.

"Yeah? Well, maybe I do want to. Is that so wrong? Maybe I've been stuck taking care of everything forever and I'm sick of it! Everything and everyone and never being able to do anything I wanted to. Do you realize that I was younger than you are now back when Dad left? It all just got dumped on me. And just when things were getting alright, what happens? That stupid car accident, and then I had to do even more." He stands up. His face is red and he roughly wipes under his nose. He covers his eyes with his palms and leans back. I continue to inch away as he turns back toward me with his hands on his hips and yells,

"It's your turn now, Vic! I get a break. I get to not take care of anyone but me for like five minutes. You. You get to grow up and do it all for a change." His friends walk out of the front door and flank him on the porch. I look from one to another, feeling like a deer facing a pack of wolves.

I place the case on the ground and reach down for pieces of broken asphalt. Throwing it at them, I scream, "Why are you helping him? He's leaving all of us." The chunks fall far short of the boys. Picking up the case, I turn to run.

A low growl escapes Dan. The boys run after me without speaking.

Go! my head screams. I lock my gaze on the hole in the oleanders. The suitcase smacks hard against my shin and I whimper. I hear them. Feet thump and slide toward me. I'm not very far away when one of Dan's friends passes me and turns to block my escape. I veer away from him, but my feet slip and I'm sent twisting in the dirt. I turn to get up, but Dan grabs the edges of the suitcase. I pull back on the suitcase, wedging my hands and wrists into the handle to keep it from him. The suitcase bursts open and the contents are dumped on my legs and the street.

"Victoria, what the hell? Look—look what you did!" Dan's yelling now, his voice touched with a warble. "No more. No more. No more." His friends come over and they all throw his clothes into the open case. He puts his hands on his knees and takes a few deep breaths before looking up at me again. "Victoria, stop running. You can do this and I have to go."

We stand and stare at each other as all of the clothes are put away and the case is snapped shut. I nod and stare up at the sky. Warm trails are created on my cheeks. I want to tell him I'm scared, but I can't find the words. I hear them in my head but can't get them out of my mouth. I meet his gaze and his face softens. He opens his arms and, still nodding, I walk into his sweaty embrace. Safe. For this moment I feel safe.

His friends walk ahead of us, squeezing his suitcase into his stuffed trunk. Dan lifts my chin and dries my face with his thumbs. He smiles at me and I smile back as best I can. He's going. He's really, really going. Dan drapes his arm across my shoulder as he walks me slowly down the driveway. The closer we get to the car, the tighter his arm pulls me to his side and the longer it takes for one foot to pass the other. I look up at him and realize it's hard for him, too. Somehow that makes it a little easier.

"You know, Victoria." He looks over at me and smiles. "You can call me anytime. And now that I'm out of the way, guess who gets to make the rules?"

"Me?"

"That's right."

We jump in the car and head to our antique shop. Mom is talking to a couple of out-of-towners, and I figure out quickly that they're trying to get her to come down in price on a set of china. Mom looks up at us hopelessly. She can sell, but she can't barter. A wave of guilt washes over me. I didn't call anyone to help her. They're talking too fast and she's getting confused. She's my responsibility now.

"You know," I say, walking over. "That set's pretty rare. We bought it from a couple who met while working on trains and retired up the street from here. This set is authentic Union Pacific Winged Streamliner china." I know about the china. I know about everything in this store. "Used, but not much before they were retired. Look at each of the plates: they're in great shape, with minimal damage to the design in the middle. There are no cracks. At this price," I point to the card I made about it with the price clearly marked on top, "it's really a bargain. Bring this up to Los Angeles to sell and you'd make a nice profit. Or keep them. They're a great investment." I stand up to my full height and look from one set of eyes to another. I keep my face passive and elegant like my dolls. They won't rip us off. I won't let them.

After a couple of minutes in hushed conversation, the couple buy the china and I wrap each piece carefully. They're delicate. They're important.

Mom hugs Dan goodbye as the couple walks out of the store

with their new treasure. I grab a bottle of Windex and a squeegee from behind the counter before going to hug Dan goodbye, too.

"What's that for?" Dan points at the bottle and I nod toward the front of the shop.

"The windows. Now that I'm in charge, I want to have clean windows."

15

HONEY WIND - CORNELIA FEYE

The honey wind blows the curtains into the room, where I am trapped. They bunch up like a parachute in descent. Meltemi, the honey wind, licks up in the afternoon, starting gentle; later, it attacks with the ferocity of a wild game hunter. White sheets drying on clotheslines feel its fury. Clothespins save them from sailing to the street below. I wish I could sail with them. Suddenly, the wind changes its tune; sharp flapping turns into a hum like that of a bumblebee.

Turtle doves gurgle close by; a Vespa passes in the narrow lane below, its engine amplified by whitewashed walls. If only I could escape on its backseat. The island is resting at this hour, siesta time, but I am restless. Close by, the horn of a ferryboat blares in the harbor, on its way to the port of Piraeus. That's where the incident happened as I ran to catch a boat to Naxos. The reason I am a captive, listening to the wind and the turtle doves.

The sea is a hundred feet away, but unreachable for me. Downstairs a woman clatters with pots and pans. A phone rings. The woman's voice answers lazily. I want to call out *Please help me*, but I don't speak Greek. Through the balcony door I see a white wall. Stark sunlight casts one half into shadow; the other half is blinding white. Black and white separated by a sharp line. Nothing happens and still so much is going on. The incident determines my day, all I cannot do. The farthest I get is the east balcony in the morning and the western one in the afternoon. I see houses on both sides, and a slice of dark blue sky overhead. White and blue, the colors of Greece. For too long I have taken my freedom for granted, exploring, traveling the world. Now I am stuck in this room, on a Greek-island Sunday afternoon. I don't allow my thoughts to run ahead, to the outside world I cannot reach. Right here and now birds are twittering. I can't see them, but I know they're there.

Across the lane, a balcony runs along a building. An old woman dressed in black walks back and forth until darkness falls, until her family calls her for dinner. Each day she passes the afternoon hours like that. She, too, is a prisoner of her second-floor apartment. I try to catch her eye. *We are in this together*, I signal desperately. But her glance does not stray; she looks straight ahead, continues walking, putting one foot in front of the other carefully. Of course, she is much wiser than I. If I had done what she is doing, I would not be lying here.

Instead, I slipped on a wet iron ramp and broke my leg. Now it rests in a white splint, red toenails wiggling, the only part of my leg that moves. My toes and the honey wind.

16

MOTHER LOVE - TABATHA TOVAR

The container of pills falls from Vanessa's hand and rolls across the discolored and chipped linoleum of Mother's living room. She leans down, looking under her Mother's mother's hospital-style bed, and stares at the little white circles spread in an arched line away from the container. She sees them as soldiers escaping an enemy's prison. Most of the pills remain in the prescription bottle. Waiting. *Those guys. They must have lost the will to run.* She sees them, little men trapped in a foreign cell, looking at the open lid and feeling the futility of trying to leave.

"Holy crap. You can't even do that right," barks Mother, and Vanessa startles, the pills turning back into what they are— little white circles of medication to help an old woman in pain get through another day. "Well? Pick them up."

Vanessa, younger but not young, strains to reach down to capture each of the escapees. They are just out of reach and an old terror flares up her spine, pushing her to the ground to fix the mess she created. She wants to clean it up. She must. Her breath comes in short, shallow pants. She remembers Mother as she once was, towering over Vanessa's five-year-old frame in this same room and screaming, "Look at this shit, girl! Clean up your damn mess." Dolls on the floor – half-dressed in their finery. The mess. Coloring books spread out on the carpet, one crayon reclining in the spine. Homework. Mess. Mother's rage took up all the space in the room, knocking over glasses and throwing books against the wall while Vanessa cringed in the tiny space she created with knees pressed sharply into cheeks, face flattened on the carpet and fingers jammed into her ears. She'd stay there, heart pounding, waiting for the yelling to end and the crashing to begin and the inevitable sting of palm or fist. And here she is again, on hands and knees in front of Mother, leaving a mess. Unbearable.

And yet. Vanessa fills her lungs and holds in the air a minute before rolling to her side. She stares at her hands. A woman's hands. She's not small anymore. In fact, she's bigger than Mother. Stronger. Auntie spent years teaching Vanessa to use her breath to slow her heart's racing when faced with Mother's anger. As she calms, the smell of the room changes from the rum of her childhood to a more antiseptic sort of alcohol used by Vanessa and visiting nurses to keep the equipment and Mother clean.

She rights the bottle and takes one of the escapees between her fingertips. The corners of her lips turn down as she drops it back into the bottle, listening to its sad little thump as it joins the others. Mother squirms in the bed and Vanessa's heart jumps. She silently mouths "sorry" to each of the pills as she picks them up one by one and drops them back into their container. Mother sighs. It's the irritated sound she makes before she yells. *But if I stay down here long enough, maybe Mother will forget what she'd asked me to do.* If Vanessa stays down amongst the dust and pills, she may become invisible and Mother will move on to just complaining again and everything will be all right.

But Mother doesn't forget. Mother doesn't just move on. Mother wants to kill herself and asked Vanessa to help her. Rather, Mother is waiting for compliance. "No, I don't just want one of them," she had said when Vanessa held out her morning medication. "All of them. Give them all to me this morning.

Then you can wait around to make sure it's done and you'll finally be free of me. It's what you always wanted, right? Kill me and you can just leave."

Leave? Vanessa had glanced over to the front door. It was closed. Locked. And while it's a simple thing to turn a latch and let a door swing open, her repeated attempts as a child had taught her otherwise. Sooner or later someone would latch their fingers around her arm and drop her back here with a sad little thump. *There is no leaving.*

"What are you doing down there?," calls Mother from the bed. The bed jiggles and Vanessa presses herself closer to the bottom of its frame to stay out of Mother's field of vision.

"The pills. They're everywhere. I need a minute to get them all." Vanessa flattens herself to the ground. She looks up at the silver railing that keeps Mother from falling out. *Maybe I could just pull that down? Mother could roll to her death all on her own.* She looks back toward the floor, driven by the image of Mother's rage-face popping over the railing to find her. Mother can't, of course. She's stuck in bed and needs to push a button to allow herself to sit up. Logic alone doesn't calm Vanessa's heart. She holds her breath again and slowly lets it out. *It would be easier if she were gone.*

For years, Vanessa's life has become a repeating pattern. While not enjoying the routine, its predictability provided some comfort. After work, she fed Mother a dish of soft food with watered-down vodka. Mother needed to be turned and changed at least once a night. In the morning, Mother liked scrambled eggs with her dark beer and pain pills. After Vanessa ate her own breakfast with a daily serving of insults, she was relieved by an elder-care worker or nurse and found respite at work. As a cashier, she scanned large containers of toilet paper and over-sized bags of popcorn, all the while peering into customers' faces to find those whose expression reflected a life similar to her own. There were many.

"Hiding under the bed again, Vanessa? It was ridiculous when you were a kid and is even more pathetic now." Mother pushes the button to lower the bottom part of the bed. Vanessa knows she is trying to smash her.

"Do you want me to find all of the pills, Mother? Some are really far under the bed, but if you like, I can just leave them there."

"Mocking me? Do you enjoy making fun of a helpless old women, girl? There was a time when you knew some respect. I guess that sister of mine did a good job at poisoning you against me. Even so, I deserve respect from you. It's the least you could do after all of those years I sacrificed to raise your sorry ass. You are so ungrateful!"

All those years?

Vanessa's first ten years of life consisted of drifting in and out of Mother's care in this house. Bundles of memories, tied up and hidden, shift in Vanessa's head, scattering across her consciousness. She remembers a younger version of Mother in this same living room back when it had carpet and a couch. Mother sat on the couch watching TV and drinking beer while Vanessa played on the floor out of sight. When Mother's friend came over, Vanessa was locked in her room or outside. She remembered eating peanut butter from the jar when Mother was gone for days at a time. She had to push the chair to the counter to reach it. When she was older and tall enough to get to the cabinets, Vanessa made herself cereal for breakfast with the creamers Mother stole from Denny's. Her best memories were from the peaceful weeks when Mother was gone. On those days she'd walk to school early enough to eat there. And there were the times she had to step over Mother on her way to school because she'd fallen asleep on the ground by the front door, keys still in her hand.

Most of Mother's boyfriends ignored her or locked her out of sight. But Marcus, the only one who talked to Vanessa, called Child Protective Services, and finally Auntie took her home for good. Auntie taught her that sometimes jigsaw puzzles left out aren't worth crying about. A crayon dropped on the floor was not an emergency. Auntie sat, smiled, and stayed soberly awake for Vanessa's graduation from high school and then college, her wedding and the birth of her son. It was on Auntie's lap that Vanessa laid her head and cried over a marriage dissolved and a son moved away.

Then there was the accident. Mother and Auntie sitting as equals in the front of the car. Mother driving. Drunk. They were most likely fighting as they turned right and merged with the freeway. Vanessa imagined that Mother was repeating her tired monologue of "you're turning my kid against me" and "I was always second- fiddle."

When she arrived at the hospital, Vanessa knew it had to be a mistake. How could Mother have survived but Auntie not? They were identical twins, so most people found them hard to tell apart. Maybe the police got mixed up. Why was Auntie wearing Mother's clothes? How? It was impossible that the universe was so cruel. How could Mother's lap be the one left to lay one's head upon?

Mother survived, but her legs no longer gave support. The doctors suggested she might gain some mobility back in her hands, but her hands would not listen. They remained stiff – fingers glued to each other and only able to flap back and forth. She could feed herself with adapted utensils – sliding her finger into a loop that held it to her hand. No fine motor skills. She could hold a beer but not make a phone call.

Mother rented a hospital-type bed for her living room and caretakers moved into her bedroom. Day and night there was someone to get this and clean that for her. People to yell at and cry to about the sister who never cared for her and the no-good daughter who barely helped. But when the money ran low, the caretakers stopped staying over. When the money ran low, the daughter collected the pieces of her shattered life and fit them back into her tiny childhood bedroom. Meals got made, laundry got done, and Mother was given her beer and her pills.

"Vanessa!" There is no more patience left. There's a mess in Mother's house and she needs it cleaned. Time's up. Vanessa's been found. "Do I have to go down there and get those pills myself? Throw me on the ground— you know you want to. Throw me on the ground and I'll just lick them up. I don't need you."

Vanessa caps the bottle, the pills lying hopelessly back inside. Little white pills to make Mother feel momentarily better, or at least not so bad. But Mother wants to finally feel nothing at all. *At what expense? Would the police say I killed her?* Letting Mother kill herself won't bring Auntie back. They can't change places, and perhaps Auntie got the better end of the deal. Suffered less. *Mother is suffering.* Vanessa holds the bottle in her hand, resting on the floor a while longer to think about the choice in front of her. To end suffering is a great gift, and the cost of that gift would be the penalty of matricide. Would she be sent to jail? Would mother Mother find this just? The world would be cleaned of them—of them both.

"Finally," Mother says as Vanessa gets up and sits back on the chair, pill bottle in hand.

"You want me arrested? For your murder?" Vanessa sits tall in the chair. Her heart beats calmly.

"My murder? I just want to finish this... . . . this... . . . horrible way to live." Mother glares. It's all she can do these days.

"But if I give you these pills, I'll essentially be killing you." Vanessa rests her hands in her lap. It almost startles her to realize that Mother, when she really looks at her, is quite small.

"Ha! You started killing me the day you were born—loud and dirty and demanding. This is just you finally paying me back. Finally letting me be."

"Is that what I'll say to the police?" Vanessa sits back in the chair. *If Auntie had lived, she'd be small now, too.* Vanessa closes her eyes a little and imagines how she'd feel it if were Auntie in that bed. *Sad. It'd be sad, and I would never want to leave her side.*

"Seriously? You see what my life is like—day after day after day in this damn bed or that damned wheelchair. You see my suffering and you just laugh at me—you run off to work and probably tell everyone how you're a little saint and your mom is so pathetic." She raises the head off her bed to better look at her daughter. "If you're so scared, give me a beer and open the bottle and go off to work. I can still hold a beer, you know. All you have to do is give me the open bottle of pills and I can pour them into my mouth myself. Then, you can wash your hands of me."

"And what if you don't die? What if you try to take the pills but they fall to the ground again and I'm not here to pick them up? What if you only take enough to make you gag and vomit and shit your pants and you have to lie in that until the nurse shows up at noon? You'd be such a mess, Mother." Vanessa feels her shoulders relax. She feels an inexplicable calm.

"You're horrible." Mother slams her arms on the bed beside her and stares up at the ceiling.

"I was never under the illusion that I am a saint."

"It was your aunt. She twisted you. You used to be so good. You used to do what I said and even loved me, I suppose."

Vanessa watches a tear seep through the valleys of skin around Mother's eye and travel over the cheek to lose itself in Mother's ear. Wasn't that caring—or something close to it? A sign that something existed within, not just the loudness on the outside?

Mother turns to looks at Vanessa again. She opens and shuts her mouth a few times as if shifting words around until the desired one is on the edge of her lips, to spit, "You should see your face. Your stupid face." She turns away and adds, "You know you look like me. You have my same stupid face. Maybe someday you'll be this lucky." She raises her half-dead hands at her daughter and then drops them heavily back to the bed. "Just give me my goddamn pills."

Vanessa sighs, her shoulders rounding as her head hangs closer to her chest. *Deep breath. Hold it. Let it out slowly.* She sits up and leans toward Mother. "Okay. Open your mouth." Vanessa drops one pill into Mother's mouth. The mouth stays open while Mother's eyes shift from the ceiling to her daughter, over and over, before closing and swallowing the pill dry.

"Are you giving them to me one at a time? Give me them all.

Just dump them in." She opens her mouth again, a baby bird demanding more from its parents. Vanessa tilts her head and smiles a little down on Mother. She twists shut the lid and stands to put the bottle back high up on the bookshelf on the other side of the room. Mother screams from her bed, "Do what I told you, Vanessa! Give me all my pills."

Instead, Vanessa walks back to her mother and double-checks the bed's safety rails.

"You coward. Give them to me." Mother pounds her hands on her mattress. "Look, did I hurt your feelings? Okay, I'm a bitch, I'm sorry. Now, just open the bottle and give them to me. Then you can leave."

Vanessa stares down at Mother for a while. There were still a few things that reminded her of Auntie left on Mother's face. The hair was once the same color, too, though in the years since Auntie's death, Mother's hair had whitened and lost some curl. *If Auntie were here, her hair would be white too. Their eyes are the same, though. If I just look at her eyes, it's so easy to imagine that she's Auntie.*

"I'll call around today. I'm sure that there is a nursing home somewhere that can take you. I'm sure I can rent this place out to pay for it. It'll be nice. Fresh start for us both. I'll try to find some place with a view of the canyons. Remember the long walks we used to go on in the canyons, Mama? Do you? It smelled like salt and sage. I would run ahead to find cool rocks and sticks. Then we'd sit under a tree and you'd help me build a village with them." Vanessa brings her fingers to her lips, remembering the heat and dust and how happy she'd felt. "I hated how you kept putting sunscreen on me, but now I know you just did that because you loved me."

"What are you talking about?" Mother looks over at Vanessa, confusion written clearly on her face.

Vanessa ignores her and continues. "Then you'd find a stick and we'd pretend it was a villager walking around my town. Remember, Mama? We used to have such fun. Being with you in the canyons was like walking out of a cave and feeling the warm sun on my back for the first time."

"Why are you calling me Mama? You never called me that. What is wrong with you?"

"Oh Mama, I'll be sure to bring you ice cream every Sunday. Remember when you'd take me to get ice cream on Sundays after church?" Vanessa smiles. She loved going to the ice cream shop with Auntie.

"We never went to church!" A red flush creeps up Mother's neck and face.

"And I would pick your ice cream flavor? Of course, I thought I was a genius by getting exactly the right flavor and totally missed that the whole way there you were setting me up." Vanessa laughs at the memory. She feels taller. Lighter. She has the sensation of Auntie's arm draped across her shoulder. She changes the pitch of her voice to mimic Auntie. "'Look, Vanessa, doesn't the cloud look like vanilla? I wonder what the cloud would taste like—maybe with some strawberry swirls! Wouldn't that be yummy?' And when I got you vanilla with strawberry swirls you'd act so surprised and delighted. You'd tell me that because you loved me so much I must be able to read your mind."

"Shut up, Vanessa."

"It'll be great. Sundays will be our special day again. We'll have a little ice cream party and reminisce about my *happy, happy* childhood with you."

"I hate you."

Vanessa's legs rest against the bed's safety rail. She leans over so her face towers above Mother's and looks directly into the small, old woman's eyes. "I know." Her voice comes from some place lower than usual. Deeper. The truth, once spilled, was not as scary as her imagination had made it out to be. Mother doesn't love her. Never did. But Auntie, Auntie-Mama, did, and that was enough. She smoothens her clothes with her dry palms and reaches into her purse to pull out her long-neglected lipstick and a small mirror. "I've always known. And someday, if I'm lucky, you won't have the energy to speak any more and I can sit by your bed and pretend you are the woman you killed in the car 'accident.'. I'll feed you and brush your hair and remember the parts of my life worth remembering." Vanessa opens the mirror and applies the lipstick. She puts it back in her purse, spilling out some gum wrappers and receipts. She straightens up and returns her gaze to her mother. "The parts that don't have you in them."

"Give me the pills," Mother whispers. Whines.

"Mother, I can't do that! Think of the mess!" Vanessa grabs her purse off of the chair by Mother's bed. Her fingers twitch to pick up the receipt and gum wrappers, but she just shakes her hands and leaves them. She picks up the TV remote next to the bed and turns on a show but doesn't wait to see what is playing. Slowly, she walks to the door without turning around. Her hand is steady as it reaches up, unlatches the door, opens it, and leaves.

THE BOX - MAX FEYE

BASED ON AN ETCHING BY SUSANNE MUEL

Something lurked in the man's dark room, waiting for him to come home from his date that night. He had first felt its eerie presence while cleaning his room in anticipation of a female guest. He knew *something* was there, he just had no idea where. After all, there weren't many places for something to hide in his bare room. He had no closet, dresser, couch, or desk. The only reasonable place *it* could be was under his king-sized bed, hidden by a gray bed sheet, where he kept most of the things he owned in an organized system of labeled plastic bins. And just to be safe, he had even checked down there. It wasn't in the bin for the jeans, or the bin for the socks and underwear, or the bin for the Hawaiian shirts, or the bin for the self-help books, or the bin for the skincare routine, or the bin for the laundry, or the bin for smaller, unused bins. Whatever *it* was, it was definitely not down there. His other possessions– the red landline phone by the wall, the geometrically patterned Navajo rug perfectly parallel to the bed, and the mason jar, used as an ashtray– provided no hideouts either.

Even so, when he walks down the hall later that night with a woman in tow, he has the sinking feeling *it* is still there. He opens the door and a brilliant light floods the room from the hallway, and he quickly peers around for anything out of the ordinary. But everything in his room is exactly the way he left it. Reassured, he holds open the door for the woman, who smiles politely as she slips her handbag onto the ground. The door shuts behind them and everything returns to darkness, so he quickly goes to switch on the light— but she tells him not to. A tickle of fear flirts in his stomach as he watches her explore his dark room, inspecting his possessions. Nervous anticipation grows inside of him, and he grins when she pulls out the red rose she bought earlier from a peddler at the bar and slips it into the mason jar. She turns and hurls herself onto the bed with a sigh and the binned items below shudder. He eagerly takes off his jacket and hangs it up while she removes her black boots, pulling them off with such force that they soar across the room.

They lie down, staring at each other on the bed. The man flinches, ever so slightly, when she removes his glasses. Without them, his vision descends into dim fuzziness. She tosses the glasses aside, onto the floor, and he can't help but wonder if they might've cracked. Her depthless, moon-like face grows closer, and they kiss. He tries to focus on her smooth lips, her warm skin rubbing against his, her faint sighs of pleasure. But when she bites his lip too hard and he tastes coppery blood, *it* floods back to his mind. She pulls away, her face a series of pooling black pits, and his stomach tightens. Her blurry body shifts as she silently sheds her clothes. He follows her lead, but wonders again: did his glasses crack?

They writhe naked on the bed, slithering into a messy knot. Her faded jeans hang off of the foot of the mattress, striped pink socks still stuck inside. Her beige bra and black panties have disappeared into the bed sheets. His clothes are sprawled over the Navajo rug. He peeks through half-closed eyelids at her giant face while her hand starts rubbing his crotch, but all he can think about is putting everything into the laundry bin.

Time passes, nothing happens. *I'm tired,* she says, and the knot untangles. She takes off her wristwatch and tosses it onto the ground before rolling over with her back to him. In the emptiness that follows, there are a million things he wants to say, but they're all wrong. Instead, he settles for silence, shifting onto his back and staring into the abyssal darkness above him. The only sound in the room is from the watch. Each sharp tick announces another moment that the woman falls deeper into sleep. When she finally does, he will be left alone with *it*. The very thought sends horrible shivering through his body as ancient reflexive responses flood his bones. He can feel *it* looking right at him. He tries to close his eyes, but the lids are stuck wide open. He's forced to stare into the motionless darkness above, a bottomless black lake, *its* monstrous silhouette hovering right beneath the surface. His heart throbs in panic, and he wants to run, to scream, to shake the woman awake, to do anything else other than look at *it*. Too late. Powerless, he falls toward the surface and sinks into the unspeakable place below, the darkness swallowing him whole.

∼

He remembered laying in bed, wide-awake in the dark. It was the first time he didn't have the comforting glow of a nightlight illuminating in his room. Dad had insisted on it. Big boys don't use nightlights, he had said. Mommy didn't sing him to sleep anymore either, because Dad thought he was too old for that too. So he stared with absolute terror into the swirling darkness all around him, trying his best to be strong, but every fiber of his being wanted to flee to his mommy's room. He could feel something lurking under his bed, waiting for the moment his foot touched the cold wooden floor. If he pulled the covers over his head and didn't move, it would go away, he thought. But that only allowed it to come closer. Its icy, scaly body crawled up his legs, over his body, clawing for his throat so it could eat him alive. Paralyzed and choking on tears, he had no choice but to sink into the only shelter left.

The Box.

∼

The man opens his eyes, but they might as well be closed, because the darkness around him is complete. For some reason, his mind is now calm, and his heartbeat still. Wiggling his toes, he discovers his body can move again. Sitting up, he lets his eyes adjust to the murk until the familiar dark shapes and outlines of his room reappear. He stands up, feeling rejuvenated. Whatever *it* was, it seems gone now. He picks up his glasses and puts them on, noticing they are uncracked. He can now clearly see the sleeping woman on the bed, and he is struck with an over-whelming urge for her to leave. He wants to clean his room again, to pick up her crumpled clothes, her bag, her dirty boots, her annoying wristwatch, and the drooping rose in the mason jar and throw them all into the hallway. He glances at his own clothes on the rug, wanting to throw them in the laundry bin. But fluttering tightness grips in his stomach, warning him of what will happen if he does. All of the clothes seem armed with a hidden security system, ready to be set off with the slightest touch. He can't risk it. Moving anything and waking her up is out of the question.

The red telephone begins to ring, shattering the silence, and he scrambles over in a panic, managing to pick it up after one-and-a-half rings. Helplessly, he glances over to see the woman stir. She slides onto her stomach, stretching, readjusting her face so it's facing him. But miraculously, she doesn't wake up. He deflates, holding the phone up to his ear. It is most likely a tele-marketer from India, or a Nigerian prince requesting help exporting his oil. Those bastards don't care about time zones, and they'll keep calling until you deal with them.

The scratchy voice on the other end is almost imperceptible, hovering at a level just above a whisper. It sounds like the call is coming from the middle of the storm, and grating white noise blares through the receiver. *Get outside your box*, it says, reading from some faux-conversational pitch sheet, aiming to sell a time-share for an eco-resort on some unpronounceable beach in Hawaii. It promises the package deal: unlimited mint mojitos, shifting grass skirts, sand so fine you can swim through it, all-you-can-eat oysters with the pearls still in them. *What is wrong with you people?* the man whispers. *It's the middle of the fucking night!* The voice licks its lips, undeterred, reading down the list of the other heavily discounted options: the Tomb of the Buddha's Fingernail in Thailand, Tours de Revolución in Chile, The Great Drag Scene of Montreal, The Prince of Kenya's Private Zoo. How about the Authentic Navajo Experience Free from White Guilt? The man glances at the colorful rug beside him, noticing creases where the woman stepped on it. *Do me a favor,* the man hisses quietly. *Go fuck yourself.* Immediately, the noise on the other end surges, getting louder and more chaotic, like a hundred garbled demons. *I hope it eats you alive,* the static says. *You won't escape it this time.* The man hangs up quickly and pulls the cord from the wall.

Shivers flood the man's body, sending goosebumps all over his bare skin. Telemarketers always make him tense. His stomach clenches tighter then before, and he suddenly feels the pang for a cigarette. He silently crawls over to the bed, lifting up the grey bed sheet to pull out the self-help box, where he keeps his cigarettes. Staring into the blackness underneath, he hesitates for a moment, before reaching his arm under and grabbing the box. But as he slides it out, he feels his arm graze against *something*. Something cold and scaly. Something moving. He quickly rips the box out and scoots backward toward the window, glaring at the little dark slit beneath the bed. His body freezes, as he expects something to slither out. But nothing in the room moves. Grabbing the mason jar for his ashtray, the dying rose inside, he opens the small window, letting in the crisp city air. He lights a cigarette, its small comforting sun floating just beneath his nose, and he takes the smoke into his shaky lungs as deeply as he can. When he exhales, beady eyes stare at him from under the bed. *It's* watching him.

He drops the cigarette in fear and quickly scurries to the bed, sliding into the covers. Chills runs through his body as he lies next to the sleeping woman, knowing what is underneath them. He is dying for sunrise, or to turn on a light, or to get her out. All of them will make *it* go away. Freezing, he listens intently for any sound under the bed. Even over the gushing heartbeat in his eardrums, he hears *it*. The undeniable sound of *something* sliding, emerging out from beneath the bed.

He can hear it moan as it creeps out onto the floor below him. It knows he's awake, so it climbs the woman's wrinkled jeans like a ladder, coming up onto the bed. He feels his body begin to petrify, and the ticks of the woman's wristwatch remind him he only has a few seconds left. But he has to wait for the last possible moment. A sudden mistake now means being devoured alive. It slips under the blanket, its cold, fleshy belly moving up his leg, creeping over his navel and up to his heart. Wherever it touches him, it leaves deadening, throbbing cramps in its wake. Right when he feels it reach his throat, he springs to life, grabbing it with both hands just beneath its massive head, not daring to look while he wrestles its squirming length down onto the floor and into the laundry container beneath the bed. It hisses, spasming amongst the dirty clothes, spraying its venom on the plastic, attempting to break free. Still sleeping, the woman turns over, covering herself with more blankets. He looks at her with disgust. She is completely unaware and ungrateful of his heroics and their narrow avoidance of death.

But the man knows any heroics are temporary. It will escape over and over until he looks upon its nightmarish form. But doing that is no different from getting eaten alive. With what little strength he has left, his failing body filling up with nausea and spasms, the man crawls back up onto the refuge of the bed. Soon enough, the jeans, underwear, Hawaiian shirts, moisturizers, and self-help books are awoken by all the commotion. As *it* throws itself against its plastic cell, they are inspired to join suit. They rattle so violently against one another that the lids of their containers pop off and they climb out. Now free, the horde spreads outward, stomping over the Navajo rug, colonizing the pristine floor. The man's possessions sprawl across the room, squirming and climbing on top of each other to claim the freshest air above. The room descends into utter chaos.

The man, quarantined to his king-sized island, feels paralysis set in again. Despite being disconnected, the phone begins to ring once again, slightly muffled by unread books and aging take-out containers. The floor is a graveyard of decaying roses. *It* emerges again from under the bed, moaning louder as its body, eyes, and teeth swell and multiply to fill up the entire room. He glances over at the woman, the one place *it* isn't, as his throat swells up and tears stream down his cheeks. He desperately wants to ask her for help, but nothing in the room terrifies him more than her peaceful sleep. So he has no choice. He sinks down, past the bed sheets, and retreats noiselessly into the Box.

The walls of the Box press tightly against him like a cold hug. As a last desperate escape into the nothingness, only the abyssal dark and peaceful suffocation exist down here. The muted thuds of his heartbeat grow farther apart, and a gentle numbness washes over his body. He lets go of his locked up muscles, the tightness gripping his stomach, and the black weight in his lungs. His worthless body, having failed him, disappears. He could stay here forever and grow wax over his eyes and they could shoot him into space with no destination; he wouldn't care. All he waits for now is the blurry hole above him, glowing with dawn's light, to close. Once sealed in, he can be left to this immobile, removed exile forever.

The woman opens her eyes, emerging from a deep, dreamy sleep. She sits up, wiping a thin layer of oil from the crown of her nose, and looks around the silent room. The messy floor is covered in dirty clothes, toiletries, and self-help books. The man's glasses lay next to the bed, cracked. The mason jar is knocked over, a half-smoked cigarette has burned a hole into the Navajo carpet. She is relieved that the man is nowhere to be seen. She silently slips on her underwear, wristwatch, clothes, and boots. She grabs her bag and quickly moves toward the door to leave.

She looks back one more time at the strange, filthy room in the morning light to check that she didn't leave anything behind. On the bed, she notices a large hole in the sheets that wasn't there before. She walks over curiously, peeking down into it, and sees someone lying inside. He is childlike, with fragile limbs and a skinny body. His head is big, with misted eyes and a cemented scowl. She reaches down and pulls him up with ease, finding him light and soft. She spends a few minutes cradling him like a baby, until sleep finally finds him and the scowl melts away. She places him down on the bed and tucks him into the blankets, then she slowly closes the door behind her as not to make a sound and wake him up.

18

ONE SUMMER NIGHT - LADAN MURPHY

As the night drew its dark skirt on a San Diego summer twilight, a wife curled up to her husband, listening to the orchestra of crickets chirping through the open window.

"Ribbit." The dry pond in the backyard filled with unseasonal rain had brought the frog to life.

"Darn, remind me to drain the pond tomorrow," her husband said.

"You won't do such a thing. Where would the little frog go?" she said.

"But he is noisy; I can't sleep."

"You can."

～

"Ribbit."

"RIBBIT." A deep-voiced loud frog joined the symphony of soft ribbits and chirps a few nights later.

"Our frog has a buddy," she said.

"I really have to drain the pond," her husband said.

"No, you won't. We'll get used to it, I promise." She really hoped they would be able to get some sleep.

"Ribbit."

"RIBBIT."

"Shut up!" The voice of the crazy woman next door filled the air.

"RIBBIT."

"SHUT UP."

"The Crazy one is really getting into it with the frog." As much as she loved the house, she hated being as close to their neighbors as an extended arm.

The soft ribbits stopped, but the ribbiting and yelling between the loud frog and Crazy continued.

"RIBBIT."

"Just wait till I catch your sorry ass!" she yelled.

The RIBBITS suddenly stopped.

"Yah, hah, now you listen—you know who the boss is."

"I really have to drain the pond before Crazy gets more upset," her husband said.

"And if you do, I'll be upset," she said.

"Don't you remember how mad she was the time the leaves from our tree fell in her front yard?"

"She'll be over it when the frog is gone."

"In the meanwhile, I don't want to hear her foul mouth screaming over the wall."

"Why are you so scared of her?"

"Because she's crazy. Ask any of her exes."

Silence fell before a long, drawn-out "R-I-B-B-I-T" ended the argument. The frog had the last word.

⁓

The next night, the usual orchestra of the crickets was accompanied by soft-sounding ribbits.

"What happened to the loud frog?" she asked.

"Don't know. Maybe Crazy scared him off," her husband answered.

～

In the morning, the bell rang, and she opened the door to a naked wet man.

"Help me, RIBBIT," the naked man said in a familiar sound.

"Wooh . . ." Her jaw dropped, and the coffee from the smashed cup she let go splashed on her legs.

"What is happening? Are you all right?" Her husband rushed to the door.

The crazy neighbor jumped over the divider wall and closed in on the naked man.

"I told you not to move—the bathtub is filled up with cold water." Then she grabbed the RIBBITing man's arm and pulled him toward her house. "Augh, how many frogs do I have to kiss?"

The wife and her husband stared at each other as the ribbiting sound faded in the neighbor's house.

"I must be dreaming!" she said.

"I think we're both dreaming!" her husband answered.

19

TRUCKLOAD - ANDREA CARTER

I n the old brown Cadillac Eldorado, June and Minnie sped down the skinny country road lined with willow trees. June was taking Minnie away from Fred Emory, the professor Minnie did not want to sleep with anymore. Around them, farmlands of tomatoes extended toward the little town of Mayfair, west of Sacramento. Minnie's bare, skinny arms held up her shoulders like cranes' legs. Eyeliner smudged her eyes. The Sacramento Valley sunset turned a neon pink from the pesticide sprays of late April. Minnie didn't make any noise, but June counted five used Kleenexes on the seat between them.

"He's the chair of my committee, June." Minnie's long, straight black hair hid her face. "I have to drop out. I have to go work in my parents' restaurant and smell like fried chicken."

"No, you won't," said June, head administrator for the English Department at the university where Minnie worked on her dissertation, and now, she was the getaway driver.

"I just told him I didn't want to have sex with him anymore, and he said I have to change my dissertation topic. That will take forever."

June slowed the car to make the left-hand turn into town when a black truck on raised struts with a dog in the back cut in front of her. The truck-bed gate was down, and the dog paced back and forth, leashed to the roll bar above the cab. The dog looked like a boxer mix, mouth open, tongue hanging out, eyes glassy.

"These people—this is why I would buy a gun." June narrowed her eyes on the back of the driver's head. "And if I could get away with it, I'd scare Fred Emory into nothing too. Dear God." She looked at Minnie. The young woman sniffed.

When the light turned green, the truck made a U-turn and peeled away.

June knew Fred, knew he forged affairs with students like Minnie. June had been enamored once too. But that was a long time ago. Twenty-three years. After June got her BA, he promised her a good recommendation to the master's program where she now basically ran the department, even though her pay and title didn't reflect that. Fred had encouraged her until she realized he'd replaced her with another girl. June had run her course on his conveyor belt of university women. She didn't get into the master's program.

Inside the Lotus Café, June spooned lemon meringue pie and watched Minnie not eat the cheeseburger that sat in front of her. The long windows of the restaurant were open, but the ceiling fans pushed the hot air back down. Flies dive-bombed.

"Do you love him?" asked June. She sighed.

"I've read his books forever," said Minnie. "I love his mind, but he wants my body. The thing is, he doesn't get it. I adore him. I just don't want to have sex with him."

"He wants you," said June. "Like a dog." June looked down at the pie and got up.

In the bathroom stall, June sat on the toilet to take a breath. She ran her hand through her short, fine brown hair. Her white sleeveless tunic blouse stuck to her sides. Her thighs felt encased in the pantyhose under her tight gray polyester business skirt.

She put her head down. What the hell was she butting in for? Practically promising to push Fred Emory to the wall for a grad student? But too many things were too fucking unfair right now: she'd learned the cancer was back when they found a lump in her other breast, her roof needed replacing, one of her dogs was dying, and she'd just got notice that the department wasn't going to be able to do a salary increase. She stood up and straightened her blouse, rolled the killer pantyhose off, and tried to smile in the mirror. She frowned at the puffy bags under her hazel eyes, the wrinkles, her skin the color of bath powder.

Back at the table, June took a sip of her coffee. Her fresh coral lipstick marked the white coffee mug.

"He's not approving me for Orals. I'm sunk—and it's my word against his." Minnie's dark brown eyes were bottomless.

"Were you pressured to have sex?" asked June.

"I went along with it. The sex was just, you know? He was a writer who inspired me to write, to study literature. He was like my superhero."

"How did it start?" June asked.

"He helped me write this article. It was late. He seemed kind, complimenting my work. He said I was so talented. He could help me. He could tell I was lonely, and he was lonely, he said. He paid attention to me. When it got physical, it was too late to say anything. I did it. I got myself trapped."

June tried not to make a face. She couldn't eat any more pie. She had heard this story too many times. She took the young women he dumped out to Mayfair, let them cry, told them they could try to fight. But she couldn't let herself be anything more than an emotional ally.

"Now, I'm just so ashamed and embarrassed. I was so naïve," said Minnie.

"He used you. But you can't walk away from forty thousand dollars' worth of debt and a lost career."

"I feel lost. I really thought he cared for me, about me. God, I thought he loved me. How stupid is that?" Minnie stuck her fork in her glass of ice water. "You know what it makes me look like?"

June pushed the pie back. "You could try to fight him."

"I don't want to ruin him," said Minnie.

June rested her chin on her folded hands. Her eye twitched. "You just can't let him fuck you over."

Minnie sniffed and scratched her nose with a pinky finger that was so delicate June couldn't really see the fingernail.

"June? Is that you?" A curvy redheaded waitress came toward them with a coffee carafe, her ringlet hair in a pom-pom ponytail.

"Mary Anne!" June hugged the woman, whose plump arms were covered in freckles.

"June, why don't you come out here more?"

"Oh, I've had a lot of stuff going on. And the term's ending."

"I'm doing a poetry reading at the Town Hall. Please come." Mary Anne filled June's cup. Mary Anne's aquamarine eyes sparkled.

"That sounds lovely," said June. "This is Minnie. She's getting ready for Orals."

"June is the best, isn't she?" said Mary Anne to Minnie.

"I am not," said June.

"Promise me. Tomorrow, Saturday, seven o'clock," said Mary Anne.

"She dropped out," said June, watching Mary Anne head to a table on the other side of the restaurant. "Mary Anne, such a huge talent when she started her PhD. She didn't fight him. She left the program. Must be four or five years now. Married some Engineering prof. Three kids."

"I can't drop out, June."

"I wouldn't," said June. But her face tensed, since she hadn't fought Fred either. How could she have?

Minnie picked up her cheeseburger and took bite after bite.

"We can't refuse Mary Anne's invite," said June.

Minnie nodded, chewed, swallowed, and gulped more burger.

~

On Saturday morning, June drifted on the daybed in the living room. It was still so hot, but the temperature would cool in the next weeks. She felt the acid in her throat. The pie and the coffee from last night. She turned on her side, cupped the left breast. The sheets smelled of her sweat. She didn't want to do the chemo again. She heard her two dogs pant at the foot of the bed. As far as Minnie was concerned, June still had no idea how to help her. But she wanted to.

Fred Emory. June remembered him, the unkempt, disinterested half-genius—poet, novelist, and scholar. Black wavy hair. Brown, wild-horse eyes. He promised her everything in the bars at 3 a.m. He recited Dylan Thomas, and his stunning achievements on American nature writing of the late nineteenth century. He charmed her. He loved her mind, especially when they were in bed.

Even after she found Fred in bed with another woman, she thought he would at least give her a letter of recommendation, something. He said sure, as he waved her out of his office. No acceptance came. No rejection either. Her application had been incomplete. Missing a letter of recommendation. She went to the bar and went home with whoever. Got fired, ran her bank account to the ground. A girlfriend let her stay with her at the trailer park, and they suffered the Tule fog that winter in thick, men's beige woolen socks. She got a clerical job at the university and wound up right back in the English Department.

She petted her dogs. The big-headed Rottweiler named Blue barked, and the black Lab, Nell, who was dying, whined.

~

Later in the afternoon, June went to the drugstore and bought dark red nail polish and antacid. The temperature sign next to the Co-op blinked 93 degrees. June crossed the street to Sal's City

Bookstore. A couple of dreadlocked students and old hippies scanned the titles on the discount tables outside.

"Mystery? Romance?" said Sal, his denim visor pulled low on his sunglasses. "All here between the covers." He shoved a couple of paperbacks on the bargain table in front of the store, where June studied the titles.

"My offer still stands. Will you do dinner with me?" Sal said this to every woman.

"No romance for me, please." June smiled. She made Sal take her $2.50 for a worn copy of *Murder on the Orient Express*. "I should really read the new stuff." She glanced at the shiny hard-cover jackets of the faculty books in the shop window.

"All that." Sal shrugged. He left her to help an older gentleman struggling to carry three books and his cane through the entrance of the store.

June inspected the new geography book and the California watershed one, and then, wouldn't you know it, Fred Emory's newest, *Claws: Animals and Other Tales*. She'd heard about it. Short stories. One in particular about a cat who narrated a couple's desperate sex life. What did Fred Emory know about women or cats?

On her way back to the car, June spotted the black truck, the one ahead of her and Minnie yesterday. The dog sat leashed to the roll bar again. She was a mutt, too thin for a boxer. The dog bared her teeth at June. The collar pulled at the dog's neck hair, where the skin looked shiny pink and raw.

"It's ninety-three degrees! What are you doing here?" The dog stood up and whined. "Oh, sweetheart." June eased her hand up to the dog's nose; the dog wriggled and wagged her tail, nuzzling her head under June's hand. June reached for the dog's tag. "Who would do this to you?" But the dog wanted to play, and June couldn't grab her. "Okay, girl. If I see you again like this, I'll be taking you home."

∽

"I've got it," Minnie told June outside the Mayfair Town Hall building before Mary Anne's reading. "It fits right into my dissertation. Women who find spaces for their writing outside the traditional model. It was here the whole time!"

"You are brilliant," said June. Minnie was the one to fight Fred Emory.

"I need to schedule a reading on campus, get all these women in Mary Anne's group to submit their work, like, right now. We don't have a whole lot of time," said Minnie.

"I can work on getting you approved for that," said June, without wondering if she could.

Mary Anne's reading raised the hair on the back of June's neck. Her poems started out sweet—water, childbirth, nasturtiums, and farmland at dusk. But Mary Anne's poems didn't end sweet at all. A crow in the final lines of the last one beat its wings against the mother's face before she stopped breathing. Arresting. Unexpected. June looked at Minnie.

"You are amazing," said Minnie to Mary Anne after the reading.

"You came," said Mary Anne to June and Minnie.

"June's here!" a young woman yelled, carrying her baby. She waved her hand to the other women who had read at the Town Hall with Mary Anne. They were paralegals, or assistant chefs, or sold insurance, or taught kindergarten in Sacramento. Bella. Jocelyn. Amelia. Rosario. The women swarmed June as she watched Minnie talk to Mary Anne.

"Oh, my God. Fred Emory." Mary Anne lost her smile. She looked at Minnie. "Sure. I'll bring the whole group. We're a truckload."

They drove home from the reading in Minnie's old Celica past the new brewery bar. June looked out the open window as they slowed before a red light. She saw the truck and the dog, parked at the curb on the right.

"Stop the car," said June.

"What?" asked Minnie.

"I'm taking that dog."

"You can't do that." Minnie put on her blinker and slowed beside the truck. A cyclist zipped past.

"You watch me." June shut the car door and marched toward the truck. Her high-heeled pumps clopped on the asphalt.

Music, voices, and yellow light spilled out of the brewery. The dog barked at June, its face flashing in the streetlamp light and then disappearing.

"Good girl." June stood up on the curb, grabbed the truck-bed rail, and hyperextended herself to pull the leash and unhook it from the dog's collar. June's feet left the concrete as she balanced herself on the side of the truck bed. The dog scrambled and twisted herself.

"You're going to get in trouble," said Minnie, who'd left her car, flashing its hazard lights, in the street.

"Help me," said June.

"I can't believe you're stealing a dog!" Minnie shoved the gate down.

The dog leaped past June, landed in the street, turned around, and started barking. June reached out and caught her right hand in the dog's mouth. The teeth sank deep. June moaned. The dog let go, backed up, sat on the curb, wagged her tail, and whined. June jerked her hand up and down as if something were still biting it.

"Oh, my God, June." Minnie grabbed her hand.

June turned and winced from the pain. The dog ran to lick her face.

"You need to get that looked at," said Minnie.

"I will," said June. The dog licked at June's hand as they got in the car.

~

June had found a small basement classroom in the old Science building on campus for Minnie's reading. It was a Friday afternoon. There were a few rows of folding chairs and a table with a podium. The chairs filled quickly, and it was standing room only.

People came from town, from the bike shop. Lots of women, their kids, some guys, boyfriends, girlfriends. Only Fred Emory came from the English Department. Minnie had walked him over. He wore a white short-sleeved shirt and a plaid beret. He sat, smoothed his beard, and crossed his arms next to June with the boxer mutt that June named Leda. The puncture marks of Leda's teeth were still visible on June's hand as she petted the dog's patient head.

"What do you know about this, June?" Fred asked, speaking above the din of voices. He looked tired, with bloodshot eyes.

"I just got them the room, for her, for Minnie," said June.

Minnie stood at the podium. Someone hit the lights. Ten mismatched candles flickered behind. "Thank you for coming, everyone. Welcome to *Women in the Here and Now*. These are poets and writers who have built their own community, coming here today to read their work."

People started clapping.

"With the permission of the writers' collective, I will be using their works, lives, and history in my dissertation."

People clapped louder and whistled and yelled.

"I want to introduce Mary Anne and the collective," said Minnie. "This reading is a tribute to Professor Fred Emory."

He stood and bowed. He winked with all his wrinkles at June.

Mary Anne came up to the podium and cleared her throat. "This is called 'The Bite.' With an epigram from Carolyn Kizer's poem 'Bitch.'" It was so quiet you could hear Mary Anne pressing the page of her chapbook open.

The crowd roared when Mary Anne finished. The candles flickered and the flames arrowed toward the ceiling. June clapped too. The nausea she felt earlier had completely left her body. The dog tugged at her leash, and her claws scratched on the linoleum floor. As good as June felt, she was too weak to pull the dog back, and it leaped at Fred, who tried to get out of his chair. People crowded around the dog and Fred. June heard Fred cry out. Amid the buffeting of bodies and wrestling on the floor, the dog barked, and chairs got shoved and knocked over. Gradually, people stood up and backed away. In the dark, June could see the dog licking at a body on the floor. It was Fred Emory. June thought she saw blood staining his white shirt. The dog must have bit him. She wondered how deep the wound went, how much it hurt.

20

MEAT - SUZANNE HAWORTH

The diner door opened letting in a gust of damp night air. A stranger came in with it. He stood a few inches over six feet, with broad shoulders, good looking in a pale, unhealthy sort of way. Ernie glanced at Sylvia. She liked big men. Would she want this one?

Automatically, Ernie peered between the dirty print curtains to check up on Main Street. Bare October trees in the copse across the road stood ghostly frail in a thin nocturnal fog. Ernie clenched down on a shiver of uneasiness. The trouble in Ford Crossing liked the night.

Only him and Fred and Sylvia in the place. Late for dinner.

The new guy took a table at the back.

Sylvia stood at the end of the counter, one foot hitched on the rail, an elbow planted on the yellow Formica, talking to Fred. Her ripe body said nineteen years old, but her eyes held a century of experience.

She ran an appraising look over the new guy before meeting Ernie's pleading look straight on. Then she started a smile, that cat-got-the-canary smile, lips only.

He'd love to wipe that confident smirk off her face. Just once.

She crossed the diner. Unbuckled ankle boots clomped. Hips swayed, rhythmic and seductive. Apron tails bounced behind her short black skirt. So damned cute.

Not him, not tonight, Ernie shouted real loud in his mind. *This is my night.*

He followed her progress over the rim of his coffee cup. His body registered the familiar hot-cold craving. His farm-fed biceps flexed, straining the material of his T-shirt.

Sylvia stopped in front of the newcomer and pulled out her order pad with a lazy, calculating look. "Hi, how's it going tonight?" Her voice was low and husky, the most come-fuck-me voice Ernie'd ever heard. Sick with longing, he watched her lean a hip against the table preparing for the gettin'-to-know-you talk.

Same approach she'd used on him six months ago when she first hit town straight off the midnight bus from somewhere near Lake Champlain. Breezed into Fred's diner half a mile beyond the lonely end of Main Street and staked out her patch in their farm community. Changed Ernie's life forever. His stomach got tight remembering.

"The special's meatloaf and mashed." Sylvia winked at Fred, owner and cook. "Believe we could rustle up some tuna casserole or lamb stew if you prefer."

Fred gave a nod and smiled shyly with that dumb-ass vacant look he'd been wearing since she got here.

"Defrosted, no doubt," the new guy said in a deep bass rumble. "I never eat that kind of crap." His raised eyebrow matched the contempt in his tone. "I hate microwaved."

Fred looked up from filling a salt shaker. Since his skin color mimicked the army-green turtleneck he'd had on all month, Ernie couldn't tell if he reddened.

"Never dilute my protein, period. You got a fresh T-bone?"

Fred scratched his neck inside the wool collar and nodded. He wore the sweater 'cause Sylvia said she liked it. Ernie tugged on the cowboy scarf she'd given him. He felt a bit ashamed how much he treasured the shabby token.

"Better be fresh! Marbled, juicy and rare."

Ernie tried to remember if he'd ever given orders like that. Not lately for sure. Too busy trotting along when Sylvia whistled. Like Fred and a few others he could name.

Not the stranger, Ernie noticed a while later when Sylvia deposited a plate in front of the guy, rapping it down a little louder than necessary.

"Your steak, mister."

The big man didn't look up; his attention stayed on the food. He cut into the meat, face absorbed, watching the blood follow the knife and pool under the fries.

"Seared outside, raw in," she said.

The man ignored her.

Sylvia's eyes took on a harder glint than usual in the flirting stage. "Just the way I like it myself," she said.

The man passed on the invitation in her voice and put a chunk of beef in his mouth, not even giving her a glance.

"You want ketchup or A1?" Sylvia pulled bottles out of her pockets with the speed of a gunslinger. No response. The guy reached for the salt.

Ernie smiled to himself.

She tried again. "I haven't seen you in here before. You new in town, or just slow at spending your money in fancy restaurants?" She laughed a soft, mocking laugh.

The man chewed slow and purposeful-like. After what seemed a long silent time, he looked up from his empty fork to the rust-colored stains on Sylvia's apron, paused longer on the swell of her breasts under the tight V-necked T-shirt, longer still on the Hooters cleavage, and finally dragged his gaze up those last few inches to her face.

Hand on thrust-out hip, Sylvia's lips parted in an expectant smile. She flicked Ernie an impish glance and grinned. Teasing him was part of the fun.

The man's jaws worked slow and methodical, with goat-like regularity. After he swallowed, his slate-gray stare fixed on Sylvia. He spoke in an odd, raspy voice. "Just passing through.

On business."

Sylvia gave him her dimple smile. The guy was twice her weight, but she acted like she could take him easy with just her wily ways if he didn't come gentle.

You promised me, Ernie screamed silently. She ignored him.

"What business?" she asked.

The man took a pull on his coffee. "My business."

Ernie turned his half-laugh to the window before she could see it. Didn't work. He felt the flash of her temper smack the back of his head from across the room.

"You a salesman or something?" she asked the stranger.

"Or something," the man said. "Look, honey, I had a long day. I'd like a little peace and quiet with supper."

Uh-oh. Ernie sat a scant eight feet away, his cup arrested halfway to his mouth. The menace in that voice from the abyss chilled his blood.

The rest of Sylvia's usual banter stilled in her throat and the smile died out of her face. Her gaze sank to the weird, antique-looking ring on the big man's pinky. Motionless and docile, she stood like she was mesmerized or something. She stared at it so long Ernie half rose from his chair.

After a minute she tried again. "Food okay?" First time Ernie'd ever known her sound uncertain.

The guy's dark eyes, deep set beneath a high white forehead, bored into Sylvia's. Maybe he looked anemic because of the dark blue sweater, or maybe it was the black hair combed down flat. Tiny ears, close to his head, gave him a serpent-like appearance. The man stroked a finger over a brow and Ernie saw his hands were thin, the fingers long, the nails clean and painted shiny with clear lacquer. *Jesus, what kinda creep paints his nails?*

"Where'd ya get that?" She pointed at the dull gray metal with the complicated design and flashy red stone. "My daddy had a ring like that a long time ago."

"Doubt it." The new guy sucked in a mouthful of coffee. "Not like this one."

"Daddy said it held secrets."

His gaze sank back down the route—cleavage, swell, stains. Addressing the mouthful he worked onto his fork, he said, "Your apron's dirty." He shoveled steak and fries into his face. "I need more coffee." Not precisely impolite, but not a request, either.

Ernie held his breath. In the six months waiting tables at Fred's Diner, Sylvia had never been rebuffed by any man that Ernie knew of.

Her face went blank while she smoothed the flat of her hand over the marks on her apron. Then she drew in a hissing breath, like she was sharpening a sentence to flatten this bozo.

The man went real still. His eyes came straight up to hers this time and the two shared an electric moment of silence. Ernie nearly fell off his chair when Sylvia trotted right off to get the coffeepot without saying one single word and poured him another cup. Guy didn't look up, just kept chewing. Sylvia went back to the end of the counter.

Ernie shot the stranger a worried look. He was a big man and looked hard hewn. Ernie didn't want to wrestle with him. He shuddered at the memory of the two bikers last month. He set his cup down with a soft click. He'd love to leave her in it, just once.

As if she'd heard his thought—and maybe she had—Sylvia glanced over at him. Ernie slouched lower in his chair, head turtling into his shoulders. No question he wanted her, but the truth was that wild stuff scared him. Sylvia was a serious handful of a woman all right. Sometimes he hated her, but he craved her more. Ernie had no illusions. Addiction to this kinda woman was just plain suicidal.

He avoided her eye and took another squint outside. Only two vehicles by the curb, his truck and a black Mercedes. The Merc had to be the stranger's. A silver moon flew out from behind fast-moving clouds to shine briefly on wet asphalt. No traffic. No one lingered outdoors in Ford Crossing after dark nowadays. Not many in the daytime, either.

Mostly abandoned, the town rotted unhindered, a decaying

hub of emptiness. So far, no one even wanted to tear it down. A lot of people had left. Ernie'd thought of getting out too, but somehow never did. Knew in his heart he never would.

Shit. Ernie spotted an SUV with an official emblem pulling up.

Sylvia was edging in for another move on the stranger when the door pinged and Joe Grogan, the local sheriff, entered. Ernie could have done without Joe tonight coming in all blustery testosterone. A breath of gray bog mist swirled around his shiny, knee-high leather boots. Correction: mud-splattered boots. Joe'd been trackin' something in the marsh.

Rubbing his hands together, the law stopped a few feet inside and gave the room a quick once-over. He shrugged out of an orange hunter vest, revealing his badge.

"State Troopers found another one. Same as the last three. Puzzled as hell over their throats all torn out."

The stranger's eyes swiveled up to the sheriff. The three regulars stared at him too. No one said anything.

Grogan pushed a rogue lock of blond hair off his forehead. "Oh, sorry, Syl." He glanced at the new man. "Guess I was a little thoughtless."

"Asshole," Fred said under his breath, slipping a fifth of Jack out from under the counter. He turned away to take a pull before wiping the back of his hand across his mouth. Fred scuttled through the saloon doors to the kitchen. Out of sight, he rattled some pots and pans.

Ernie could picture him guzzling booze as clearly as if he had Superman vision lasering through the walls. Fred's military-related PTSD had taken a righteous turn for the worse. Poor bugger hadn't taken a sober breath in six months.

Grogan straddled a stool at the counter and called out his usual order, double cheeseburger and a beer. Fred returned from the kitchen carrying a couple of beef patties and a bottle. Grogan twisted half around to give the stranger behind him a long assessing look. Fred got busy at the grill.

In the silence, the stranger asked the room, "What other three?"

No one answered.

A crease ruffled the stranger's brow as he looked into faces that didn't look back. He signaled for the bill and drew out his wallet.

Slow as a snake in December, Sylvia walked up to his table, her eyes smoldering in that odd way of hers. The man threw money on the table. "Keep the change, honey." He nodded toward the sheriff. "What's he talking about?" Hard to ignore the command in that bottomless voice.

Sylvia shrugged.

"Anyone?"

Fred and Grogan kept their eyes on the meat sizzling on the grill, their mouths shut.

The man looked to Ernie.

Ernie winced, his stare drilling into his table.

Sylvia picked up the bills and shoved them into her apron pocket. "Thanks, friend." Her smile broadened, stretching the skin tight and translucent over those fine facial bones. She put her knuckles on the table and leaned in toward him. Her voice got real low in her throat, kind of a purr. "You gettin' interested in our little town after all?"

"Not really. Just asking. Might have some bearing on my business." He leaned back in his chair, his posture easing with the after-dinner expansiveness some men show.

Ernie watched him give her a different-flavored once-over.

The man said, "I hate small towns. Passing through them is just part of the job." The thin lips lifted fractionally at the corners. For the first time his expression warmed a little. "My mission in life, you might say, is to transform them."

"Transform them how?" Sylvia asked.

"Development. I look for possibilities. Assess. Make recommendations. If it's a go, we negotiate, renovate, update. Like a makeover." Sardonic laugh lines crinkled the skin at his temples.

His eyes scanned her body and his expression thawed another notch. "You could call me a talent scout."

"Are you planning to change *our* little town?"

"Could be. I'll take a look tomorrow. Why? You a preservationist or were you born here?"

"Nope. Just got lucky." She grinned at him.

The man glanced around the diner, his cold gaze pausing briefly on Ernie's face. Ernie's insides lurched and he looked away quickly, unnerved. His heart sank when the guy said to Sylvia, "Not much here for someone like you. Ever think of changing your luck? Pretty woman like you ought to consider moving on to a bigger challenge. Know what I mean?"

The world got real quiet.

Sylvia moved a little and managed to lean against the guy's leg. "What have you got in mind?" Her eyes skimmed over to Ernie for a moment.

Sometimes Ernie wished he had it in him to kill her, he really did.

"We need somewhere private where we can talk." The man stood up, shrugged into his jacket, and stared down into Sylvia's upturned face. "Can you recommend a place to stay?"

"Sure I can. Just up the street there's a place will suit you fine. I'll show you."

"When do you get off?"

"Anytime I want. Fred won't mind. Will you, Fred?"

With his back to the room, Fred waved a hand over his head.

Joe Grogan exchanged a frown with Ernie. Sylvia ignored them both. Her attention fixed on the stranger's broad back as he moved toward the front door. When she started after him, Grogan reached out and clamped a hand on her arm. "Not a good idea tonight, Syl. State Troopers are real worried. So am I."

The stranger paused and looked back.

Sylvia rotated her head slowly toward Grogan. He pulled his hand away.

The bell over the door pinged. The big man went outside, leaving the door half open.

By the time she got there, Ernie was blocking the exit. He hissed, "You heard what Grogan said. It's too dangerous."

"Back off."

For a moment Ernie stayed put, meeting her eyes, defying her.

The guy looked up from the sidewalk. "What's the holdup? You coming or not?"

Ernie's spurt of inner strength caved. Without another word, he unhooked her jacket from its peg and set it around her shoulders.

"That's right, sweetie." Sylvia patted his cheek. "Don't worry, I'll save you some." With two fingers, she moved Ernie aside and joined her new friend.

The guy said, "Looks like we pissed off your boyfriend."

"He'll live." Sylvia nodded at the dull amber streetlight on the road out of town. "That way."

"Looks dead down there." The stranger lit a cigarette. "We'll take my car."

"You won't need your car."

Their footfalls sounded flat in the low-lying mist.

"Where you taking me?"

"Somewhere you've never been before." She laughed softly and rubbed her body against him. "You gonna give me something to remember you by?"

The man looked down at her through the gloom. "Sure, sweetheart. You read my mind." He slipped an arm around her and drew her close. As his face headed toward hers, Ernie pounded down the steps and jogged across the street. Grogan leaned against the diner opening, arms folded across his chest, face hard, surveillance mode.

"Let's go, honey." They walked on until Sylvia made a noise —somewhere between a laugh and a croak.

Ernie, watching from the sidelines, knew the exact moment the stranger felt something on his arm he didn't expect. Understood how the guy's insides turned to ice when Sylvia moved in that odd way no man should ever feel a woman move.

Her jacket slipped to the ground and her shoulders drew up into vulture-like peaks. The new guy peered down at her. Sylvia smiled up at him. What he saw in the weak yellow glow of the distant streetlamp got his eyes real wide. Her pretty face spasmed as her jaw slowly elongated. The red lips stretched wide; the incisors grew an inch.

Ernie knew from experience that's when first-timers disintegrated from the inside out.

The guy backed away from her, one hand feeling blindly behind him.

Her claws reached for his shirt half-heartedly. Wet teeth snapped at him almost playfully. "Where'd ya think you're going, *honey*? We're just getting acquainted."

The grinding growl of her burned-sounding snarl made Ernie shudder.

Usually, she eased into the reveal so she could pretend it was a seduction. Sometimes it was. That's how she grew her fan club. Her boys. Not tonight. No foreplay with this guy.

The stranger turned toward the woods. Ernie moved out of the mist in front of him. The man wheeled around and made a dash for the diner. He raced up the steps. Grogan braced his hands side-to-side on the door frame blocking entry, his badge a dull gleam on his chest.

The man retreated slowly, inching backwards to the sidewalk. He staggered off the curb, righted himself, and slowly faced the woman-thing in the center of the street.

"What do you want?" he whispered.

"Well, hummm." She tilted her head, considering. "For a start," she croaked, "how about giving me that ring?" Her arm unfurled between them. "Brings back memories of the old days and stuff." She held out a misshapen hand. "Where'dja get it?"

"What?" His eyes fixed on the flesh of her palm. It pulsated strangely. His voice slid an octave higher, losing all that baritone authority. "M-m-my uncle bought it in a pawn."

"M-m-m, my. A pawn, huh? Doubt it." She snapped her

fingers. "Come on, come on, don't keep me waiting." Fierce red eyes compelled him to hand it over.

He tore the ring off and threw it to her. She snatched it out of the air, and for a few seconds, studied it, turning it this way and that. Finally, she shook her head and made a tsk-tsking sound. Drool fell to the ground.

"My bad, not the old family heirloom after all. Mine had rubies. This is glass." She shrugged. "I've been wrong about this before, but a girl's gotta try, ya know." She gave a snuffling chortle and stuck the ring on her thumb. "We're engaged."

The Sylvia-thing tucked her chin down, knees loose, flexed for action like she was testing out her new limbs. Her brow bone rippled a few times, then settled into an ugly bulge.

Ernie'd seen it before, so most of his attention stayed on the big man.

The stranger shuffled away from her, dream slow, his face ash white. "What *are* you?" The rich baritone broke like a sob. He looked to the diner, his eyes appealing to Grogan.

Fat chance there, friend.

Like he heard the thought, the guy's frantic gaze sought Ernie. "What is this?" Ernie shook his head. The man faced the woman beast.

Sylvia's head protruded forward on a neck now extended stalk-like, sinewy and eager. She laughed low in her throat, but it didn't sound sultry now. More like she'd dredged it up from some hell-bound void. Blood-red orbs in dark hollow sockets fixed on the man with lethal promise. Her scaly tongue poked between a vicious set of fangs, hungry, anticipating. A lump of saliva dangled from the expanded mandible.

The big man backed another step. His eyes bulged. Tears welled. He moved toward the derelict town. Ernie figured he'd make a try for his car. He coulda told him it wouldn't work.

Fred stepped out of the alley by the diner, a bayonet across his chest.

Next, just like Ernie knew he would, Sylvia's date took off running and headed straight for him. Figured he was the weak link. The big man was surprisingly fast. Ernie willed himself to stand his ground, reach out, stop him, but he couldn't do it. He froze. In seconds the guy made it over the crumbling stone wall and into the trees.

Sylvia stood stone still, letting him get through the skimpy thicket. The sap made a dash into the fallow field, but lost time looking behind himself way too often. When he got a couple of hundred feet in she went after him, slow at first, swaying, a soft growl rumbling behind the beauty-queen breasts still jutting out ahead of her. Her prey stumbled over a root and went down. In a burst of speed that always awed Ernie, Sylvia reached the guy in seconds. A couple of bounds and she sprang, her talons stretched wide.

The man shrieked.

Unwilling but ready, Ernie closed toward them, his eyes darting from one to the other. He didn't have to help her after all. The chump went down easy. He struggled at the beginning when she dug into his sweater, shredding it. Lumps of flesh came away with the material. Soon he just lay there, one hand flapping like a flaccid fin. When she tore into his chest the whimpers died away. At the end, her jaws fastened on his neck, ripping deep into the tendons.

Her legs straddled his torso like a rodeo rider on a bull. Hunched over him, predatory, intent, Sylvia fed. Her low grunts and moans sounded like satisfaction.

Hell, it must be the dark moon. Ernie got hard watching the short black skirt hitch up high on her thighs and bounce around her backside as she ate. A red patch spread like cum over the apron stains the stranger had noticed earlier. Before she finished, the cute bow loosened and the apron fell away.

Ernie's eyes glazed over while he listened to those feeding noises. They haunted what little sleep he got nowadays. Eventually, all sound stopped.

Movement at the diner window caught his eye. Behind the half-open curtains, Fred pressed a hand against the glass, fingers splayed, like he was forbidding something. The other hand tilted a bottle to his lips.

Grogan stood in the middle of Main, hands on hips as if he were about to direct traffic. His attention ranged down the street and back again.

Sylvia got up and staggered toward the road, drunk. Most of her face and chest shone dark and wet. Erect nipples stood out, clearly visible under the saturated T-shirt now molded to her body. Ernie licked his lips.

Grogan trotted across the field.

Ernie moved in to catch Sylvia before she fell, but the lawman got there first. He put one arm firmly around her waist from behind; his other held her shoulders. The Sylvia-thing lay back against him. Grogan's faced looked strained while the she-beast shimmied and jerked her bones back into their human form. The shoulders shrank down. The arms eased to normal. The claws retracted. Leg muscles juddered one final time, then let go. Her forehead rippled a few times, then subsided. Her jaw clenched in the throes of re-forming, then slackened. When it was done, she'd softened to her regular girly beauty. Her face shone with a strange light.

Grogan reached inside her shirt to cup a breast for a greedy squeeze. While he kneaded his fingers in her flesh, he looked over at the stranger.

Ernie's mouth watered while he imagined his own hands on her.

Sylvia's head, now curved smooth and pretty, fell back against the sheriff's shoulder. Blood dripped from her sweet round chin.

"Is he dead?" Grogan asked.

Asshole, Ernie thought, *just look at the fucker*.

Sylvia shrugged, yawned, and nestled into Grogan's arm, leaning against him in post-feeding stupor. Eyes closed, half asleep, she slipped a bloody hand down the front of his pants. "I hate when they call me 'honey.'"

All three chuckled.

Grogan met Ernie's eyes, then scooped her up in his arms, nodding to Ernie to let him know he'd be back to help clean up. They had to hide this one right. The way he held her said he'd be taking his time.

Ernie sank to his hands and knees and crawled forward to see what she'd left him. That terrifying, nauseating, perpetual craving screamed in his veins. The revulsion didn't stop him. Ernie gave a fleeting thought to her promise that she would be his tonight. Promises meant nothing to Sylvia. He reached for the dead man and thought of Sylvia in his arms; that silky supple flesh responding to his touch as it had that first time. The only time.

21

THE BOUQUET - JENNIFER PUN

The attack happened on a Tuesday, after work, at the cash register of Joy's Flower Shop on the corner of Fifth and University. The florist placed the finishing touches on a bouquet of peonies; red berries played peek-a-boo between the plush pink puffs. She wrapped the thick green stems in recycled brown paper and tied it with a generous length of burlap before threading one end of the cloth through the hole in the note Carl had written:

To My Dearest, Doc Molly, with love, your Carl.

The florist (her name tag read: *Joy*) glanced up at him not once, but twice, as she secured the note in place and handed him the bouquet.

Carl's cell phone buzzed; a text from Doc Molly: *Heading home.*

Joy looked up a third time. He held her gaze; he smiled, his sweet toothy smile, then pulled out his credit card from the sleeve on his phone and inserted it into the terminal.

"She's my wife," he said. "She's a veterinarian." He could almost hear the neurons in her brain fire, reassessing him from weird stalker patient to adoring husband.

"She's going to love them," Joy said. "Flowers and fruit, right? Fourth anniversary?"

He nodded.

"It's nice when guys remember."

If only he'd remembered yesterday.

A bell chimed—a high-pitched ding-ding. He'd heard the same sound when he came through the door, and so he continued to press the buttons on the card reader's keypad, taking his time to calculate the proper amount to tip. For these reasons, he didn't turn to see who entered the flower shop. It wasn't until Joy screamed—her shrill, piercing, fear-of-God scream—that he finally looked up, but by then it was too late.

~

When the zombie bit Carl's shoulder, let go, and bit down harder on his neck, he was brought back to the day when he was sixteen and Holden Kramer, the school bully, pinned him to the floor with one knee and ran the jagged edge of a handsaw hard across Carl's right shoulder. The metal dug deep into his flesh. He thought the handsaw pain was the worst pain he'd ever felt, but this gnawing, ripping, zombie-clamped-to-his-neck pain rendered him unconscious.

Carl imagined he tried to fight back. He recalled images: Joy, hands to her mouth; the wooden shelf buckling under his weight when he fell; and the thick ribbons of red his face left when the zombie dragged him across the linoleum floor. He remembered the zombie's short black hair slick with pomade and its hot breath that reeked of curdled milk and rotting meat. And he remembered the suffocating metallic taste of blood.

~

Carl opened his eyes. The flower shop was empty. Broken shelves, shattered glass, and pools of blood littered the floor. Flat on his back, he shuddered and tried to push himself up, but both elbows were stuck—one at 90 degrees and the other straight, with his hand still clutching the flowers. He pulled his knees in and forced himself to sit, then stand. His phone lay face up on the counter. With his free hand, he dialed 9-1-1 but barely finished before his fingers curled inward and stayed there. The operator answered, then asked, "What's your emergency?" He replied with snarls and grunts.

A large mirror behind the register was smashed in one corner. Spiderweb cracks sliced Carl's reflection but failed to mask the horror of his face: one swollen eye—a black and purple lump—a crooked jaw, a left shoulder shrugged high. The right side of his neck was a bloody mix of tattered shirt, ripped skin, and exposed bone. The worse-than-handsaw pain was gone, replaced by a gnawing in his stomach and an itch in his throat, a hunger he couldn't ignore.

He'd read about the recent zombie attacks in the news. When a friend posted about a cousin in Tampa turned flesh-eating cannibal, he sent his condolences. Doc Molly said the country was ill-prepared for a zombie epidemic, but annoyed with her practitioner's perspective, he dismissed her concerns. "These things happen in Florida and Louisiana and places like Fairfield, Alabama, but not here on the West Coast in Southern California."

His head throbbed. He raised his hand to rub his temple, but unable to bend his elbow, his arm rose straight up. High enough for him to see the bouquet in his hand. Most of the flowers had snapped off, while a few stubborn peonies clung to their stems. The green leaves and red berries held on along with the tag with his message, except now a splatter of blood was smeared across *My Dearest*.

Outside, sirens wailed. Flashing lights cast a disco ball of yellow and red inside the shop. Carl struggled toward the entrance, noticing for the first time his twisted left ankle that led him to drag one foot behind the other.

In the parking lot, a cop car acted as a barricade, and two policemen pointed rifles at him above the car hood. He raised his arms as best he could in a sign of surrender; he was the victim who called them, after all.

"Slowly," the voice blared through the cop car's speaker. "Drop the flowers."

He tried to uncurl his fingers, but they might as well have been stone. He shook his arm to release the bouquet and heard the click of the officers' weapons.

"Stop, or we'll shoot!"

She came fast like death's shadow upon the two cops and took a large bite out of one man's shoulder. The other officer turned his rifle toward her, but she disarmed him with one chomp to his hand.

Oh, Joy, Carl thought. *The zombie got you too.*

He couldn't bear the sight of more violence, with his recent attack so fresh. Blood was drying on his shirt from dark brown to crimson red. Across the street he hobbled. Approaching strangers cried out and ran in opposite directions, which suited him just fine since all he wanted was to go home.

Hunger bubbled in his throat. The urge to pounce—to feel flesh in his mouth—nibbled at the edge of his mind. How long before he started taking bites out of strangers? All he wanted was to see his wife; to give her flowers, to make amends for the previous night when he came home drunk and found her sitting alone in the kitchen, the black cherry cake with *Happy Anniversary* in white icing she baked for him on the table.

~

Their Craftsman house with its bright yellow door sat at the end of a well-traveled street. On the lawn next to theirs stood his neighbor, Martin Gupta, his back to Carl, shears in the air, pruning his prized pomegranate tree. Deep red fruit dangled from drooping branches, ready to burst with sweet ruby seeds and juice. Martin's bald head glistened like a ripe pomegranate, inviting Carl to bite. The thought of Martin's blood trickling from the corners of his mouth, down his wet chin, ravaged his gut. Sweet Martin Gupta, the high-school math teacher and widow, whose children in their twenties were almost as old as Carl. Old Martin who had lived a fruitful life already. Surely, he would not be missed. Just a tiny bite.

Carl took a step toward his neighbor, groaning and growling, with thoughts of meat: prime rib, roast beef, filet mignon, all spicy and bloody rare. Martin turned and spotting Carl, started to wave, but stopped as Carl quickened his one-good-leg pace. Martin stumbled backwards, shears pointed at Carl. A lick, tongue on skin, what could go wrong? The more Carl inched forward, the faster Martin ran to his front door. The last Carl saw of his neighbor were the whites of his eyes and his brown pomegranate skin as he struggled behind the window to pull the drapes shut.

The scent of sweat and skin subsided and Carl, chest hollow, swayed on Martin's lawn. Each moan of remorse came out as snaps of his teeth and rapid jerks of his head. He was about to eat his friend Martin! Martin, the teacher of children, the father of three. His friend who used to bring over cold beers and his wife Geeta's homemade lamb stew when Doc Molly worked late, and Carl was home alone. Martin, the doting husband whose hand Doc Molly held as Geeta lay in hospice, the last-ditch chemo treatments having run their course. "If only I could help," Doc Molly said. As if somehow, she could rework her vet skills and take Martin's lonely heart and Geeta's cancer away. The thought of eating Martin should have filled him with guilt, but the dark cloud only hovered, kept on the periphery by his growing zombie virus. He turned toward his home, to his wife.

He was late. Late for his anniversary, late for his perfectly planned apology to Doc Molly. Inside their house, his home-made sourdough bread sat cooling on their kitchen's cooling rack, a bottle of Veuve Clicquot chilled and ready to pop in the fridge. He wore his best blue dress shirt and gray slacks and had added a thin black tie, because thin black ties were hip and at thirty-four, he considered himself on trend. In the last few months they had drifted apart, with her working late shifts and him feeling his life had plateaued. He'd started to blame her, thought he deserved more. But this morning he awoke clear headed. Realized the life they sowed together was the life he wanted to grow. Tonight was his chance to say sorry, to tell her he loved her, to show her he was still the husband she married four years and one day ago. But now his clothes lay ragged, the tie lost, his hands gray and leathery. He was her husband who wasn't a husband anymore.

At the doorway, his crumpled fist and stiff fingers made it impossible to ring the doorbell or take out his key. The best he could do was walk forward and knock on the door with his head. Each time his forehead met the wood panel, he grunted. This was not how he imagined his post-anniversary dinner.

He heard the click-clack of heels on oak floors. In his excitement, he rushed the door harder. *Darling*, he wanted to tell her, *I've had the most horrible day.*

The door swung open and there stood Doc Molly, in her pale blue doctor's scrubs, her hair tied back in a loose bun; soft skin, brown eyes, lips slightly parted. For a moment the empty hunger inside him disappeared, replaced with the feeling he'd experienced when they first met: when she was a graduate student and he worked tech support; when he thought, there was no way a girl like her would be interested in a guy like him; when he wrapped himself in the torturous thick blanket of longing.

His smile turned into two snaps of his teeth. He reached out to touch her and his hand almost swiped her cheek. She stepped back, her face reflecting her medical training, calm and in control, her lips once parted, closed. Only the slight widening of her eyes—undetectable, except for him, who knew her every motion—betrayed her.

As quickly as she'd opened the door, she closed it. The door's double lock clanked shut.

～

The curtains at his house were drawn, the lights off. The day turned to night and then morning. He spent his time criss-crossing his driveway. All around him were signs something was terribly wrong: cars parked haphazardly on the road with doors open, the occasional scream and gunshot in the distance, newly minted zombies sauntering past him from time to time, searching for more victims. He kept his eyes down and his body turned to the house. He could not afford another lapse in judgment. The itch for fresh meat grew stronger, the need for human touch slowly fading away. In all his time traipsing across the front yard, Doc Molly never appeared at the windows, but he knew she was in there; he had to find a way to reach her.

Calling out her name sounded like a cat in labor. Any loud noises or movements attracted unwanted attention. He couldn't write and he had no phone. Up above the front porch was their bedroom window overlooking their front lawn—the bright green Bermuda grass he used to weed by hand and water at night. Now, brown lumps of dirt showed where he had traveled and torn the grass up with his heel. He thought of their honeymoon in Antigua, when he drew their names in giant hearts in the sand, and suddenly, he had a plan.

～

The day dragged on like Carl's left foot. In his hand, he held the crumpled bouquet in its crinkled brown paper; the petals of the peonies had all but fallen away. What was left were withered stems starved of water and brittle leaves.

None of this deterred Carl from his quest. If anything, it made him more determined. If she could only see, he thought. See how he held onto her gift. If he could lift those dead stalks and present them to her, she would know he was there. Her Carl was still inside this zombie skin.

Over time, the outline on the ground became more prominent. The letters all connected, since he could not lift his foot. He did the best he could to spell *Doc*, though he worried it looked more like *Ooc*. His foot struck something hard in the dirt

—the edge of a blue metal box. The one he used to bury Jojo, his wife's Scottish terrier. The dog lived to the ripe age of twenty-one, but his death was still untimely, having occurred while Doc Molly was away at a conference. Uneasy on old legs, Jojo toppled down a flight of stairs. Carl rushed him to the emergency clinic, texting Doc Molly to no avail. When he finally reached her, Jojo's prognosis was grave. She had him hand the phone to the ER vet and when the call ended, the vet began the process to put Jojo down. Carl raised his voice in protest, said "she'd want to say goodbye," but the vet shook his head. "This is what she wants," he said.

Carl glanced at the front door of his house. The one he'd painstakingly painted canary yellow with white trim because Doc Molly wanted her house to feel welcoming—a warm beacon after a hard day of work—the same threshold he'd stumbled over drunk last night. Now, the door felt like a bright yellow barrier laughing at him and his inability to enter.

A creak. The door opened slowly and a figure, dressed and hooded in black, slipped out. He knew his wife's gait, the way she held her shoulders up even when dressed in sweats. The pitter-patter in his chest increased in rapid succession and he wondered if it was his heart or some kind of phantom memory. She took a few cautious steps toward him. The midday sun glinted off the object in her hand with its sharp mirrored surface and emerald handle—a Santoku chef's knife.

For months, he'd researched the best kitchen knives, perusing catalogues he ordered from Japan. Doc Molly said she was happy with the way he cooked. He said he just wanted to slice tomatoes and steak with perfection. In reality, he fantasized about a new career as a chef but was too embarrassed to tell her, afraid she'd respond with "Another career? Again?" He finally settled on the Santoku Premium 8.

His insides churned, a mix of creeping hunger and the thorny prick of heartache. The irony that she would use his knife to kill him. But could she even hurt him? He hadn't eaten since the attack. Flies swarmed the large gash in his neck, and he heard the mushy squish of maggots as they made a dinner of his flesh, but he felt no pain, at least no physical aches.

The street was quiet; no other zombies in sight. "Whrolly!" he howled. He waved the bouquet like a white flag, a peace offering to his wife.

She paused, the knife outstretched, her eyes slightly wide. He smelled her scent, her meaty, human scent with a hint of her chamomile shampoo. Drool dripped down one corner of his mouth. His feet firmly planted, bouquet extended, he willed his message to travel without words: *For you love, I love you, I would never hurt you.*

She lowered the knife in her shaking hand and took a step toward him. "Carl?"

Everything that had happened since the attack, since last night, since the few months they had been living as roommates instead of husband and wife, melted away. This was Doc Molly calling his name. He dragged his foot forward, "Whrolly," he gurgled again. He held her gaze until something hard pushed him over and a man's deep voice shouted, "Run!"

Martin sat on top of him, his hands pressed down on Carl's shoulders. "Molly! Get back in the house!" he yelled. But Molly would not budge. She stood to the side with the knife.

Since the day Holden Kramer pinned sixteen-year-old Carl to the ground, he swore he'd rise above it. He worked hard, went to community college, married Doc Molly, a veterinarian. He taught himself to play the guitar, make sourdough bread, and enjoy fine wine. He thought he needed to be something more, to be someone else, but after all he did to better himself, he was still pinned to the ground.

Carl kicked up his good stiff foot and sent Martin sailing forward. Jaws wide, he clamped down hard on his neighbor's shoulder. Martin's flesh was tougher than he expected. It reminded him of overcooked chicken. When Martin stopped moving, Carl pushed him off and stood up—a laborious, graceless task.

"Carl?" Doc Molly kept the knife to her side. "I know you can hear me. I can help; you can trust me."

Her words soothed like lemon and honey. He held the bouquet, the brown paper torn from the scuffle with Martin, and lumbered toward her, careful not to move too quickly for fear he would stumble. "Whrolly." His sweet, sweet, Doc Molly. He leaned forward to embrace her. And she raised his Santoku knife and stabbed him in the heart.

~

He remembered the taste of her skin, soft and sweet as a summer peach. In hindsight, he understood that she'd tried to help him. He knew her thoughts on suffering, had listened to her lament the limitations of pain medication and the necessity of putting animals to sleep. She stabbed him because she loved him, because she wanted his torment to end. But at the time he felt betrayed.

Now, she walked before him, jaw gnashing just like his. Her hair, no longer tied back, hung in a loose tattered mess. Her cheek had the outline of his bite mark, her blood thick in his mouth, chunks of her flesh in his teeth.

Dusk on the horizon turned the lawn violet. A sudden whiff of the living sent Carl reeling, carrying his memories away like pollen. He tried to hold onto the burnt red sky, their yellow door, Doc Molly's brown eyes, her blackened lips. He tried to hold on to the silver knife still in her hand and the blades of purple grass on their lawn. He tried to grasp every last withering thought, but what stayed with him to the end—the final fruit to be plucked— was the flutter of pink petals, the feel of crumpled brown paper, and the knowledge he'd failed at the simple act of gifting flowers to his wife.

22

BLOOD BORN - LADAN MURPHY

D awn opened her eyes. She looked around—wooden dining table, cream-colored couch—she was in her own apartment, flat on her back on the floor. A sliver of light shining through the closed curtains confirmed it was daytime. She sat up slowly, confused about what had happened.

She started to open the curtains but closed them immediately after the blinding ray of late afternoon sunlight crept from the window all the way to the couch and hurt her eyes. She sank into her seat, motionless. Last thing she remembered, she was sitting with Dimitri at the dining table when he leaned toward her, bringing his face closer to hers; she'd closed her eyes, ready for a kiss. Instead she felt his lips on her neck. Next, she woke on the ground with no Dimitri in sight.

"This was the worst date ever—I got attacked in my own apartment."

Dawn looked down at her blood-streaked white shirt. She got up and rushed to the bathroom. Her skin was pale, her hair clumped together, just above her blood-soaked shirt collar on her right side. She took off the shirt, pulled her brown hair up, and wiped off the blood with a towel. Under the dried blood on her neck, she saw two small, dark circles. She touched and massaged them but felt no pain; in fact, she had never felt more alert and alive before.

~

Just a week ago she had met the perfect man at a coffee shop. Destiny had brought her to Dimitri, no doubt about it. She never drank coffee, let alone went to a coffee shop at night. Being shy, she didn't usually talk to strangers, but the charming Dimitri brought her out of her shell. The first night they met, they walked around the same block for hours, talking. They saw each other almost every night, before she invited him to dinner at her place. Dawn had hoped this would be the start of a beautiful relationship, and now this! Dimitri was gone without a trace. She tried to make sense of it. *Had Dimitri knocked her down? Or was she attacked by an intruder? The blood could be Dimitri's; he could be hurt.* She called him several times, but he didn't pick up. She got under the hot water in the shower and washed the dried blood from her hair and her body. Putting on fresh clothes, she headed out, hoping to find Dimitri and get some answers.

As she opened her apartment door; the sun surrounded by an orange haze was sinking fast on the horizon. She heard Amy, the four-year-old neighbor kid, running toward her, screaming, "Daaawn!" Dawn knelt and opened her arms wide to let little Amy continue with her usual greeting as she flung herself into Dawn's arms. She felt Amy's tight cuddles and kisses on her cheek. Dawn closed her arms around Amy; she gave her a big hug. All of a sudden, Amy let out a sharp, loud cry. Amy's shrieking scream brought Dawn back to herself; startled, she opened her jaw clenched on Amy's neck. She tossed her head back and felt sharp fangs with her tongue. *Oh God, what have I done?* Amy struggled to get free from Dawn's arms. Panicked, Dawn opened her arms, stood up, and moved her hands to hold Amy's. Dawn sighed with relief when she saw nothing more than a red mark on Amy's neck; however, she couldn't get the desire to bite Amy out of her mind.

"We got attacked by a crow—it hit your shoulder with its beak. Let's go inside and call your mom," Dawn said.

Amy seemed to have bought her story. Sobbing, she let Dawn lead her into the apartment. The chocolate bar Dawn gave Amy did little to cheer her up. Biting the bar with rounded, pouty lips, Amy sat as Dawn looked at her neck and then down at the couch and closed her eyes. Opening them, Dawn saw the angelic round face and fair hair and realized she couldn't trust herself with little Amy. Her life had taken a dark turn into an unknown alley; what she had become weighed heavily on her heart. When Amy's mother came to get her, Dawn gave her the same story about the crow's attack.

"Those darn ugly birds, they should do something about them!" Amy's mother said. "Thanks goodness you were there. Next time she wants to see you, I'll bring her personally."

Everybody the neighborhood was fed up with the crows that descended on an empty lot nearby in large numbers at sunset. On a few occasions the birds had attacked people walking outside, but this was the first time one flew so close. *Surely, the tale of terror would be repeated throughout the neighborhood about the bird who almost flew inside* her *apartment, Dawn thought.*

Dawn sat in solitude for a while, remembering dinner with Dimitri, the blood on her neck and hair, the light through the window, Amy's shoulder, and the fang that grew and retracted. She didn't understand what was happening; she hated blood. She hated raw steak; the smell of blood made her sick.

A couple of hours later, she found herself wandering out in the dark of the night and ended up in the bar *Twilight*.

Dawn climbed on a chair at the bar, looking around. Despite the dim lights, she could see clearly all the way to the back of the bar. She listened, and could hear the people on the other side of the bar talking. She poked her finger with the steak knife and watched blood drip out—and saw the finger heal almost imme-diately. She ordered whisky and a raw steak, something she never would've done before. The drink felt warm and smooth. She tried her food, but she had to spit out the solid, unchewable piece of steak.

An arm brushed across her back, swept around her, and a hand gripped her waist. She pushed the hand off without looking at the person. The hand found its way back, landing on her waist again.

"I'm not interested," she said as she tightened her grip on her glass.

"Come on, babe." The man's sharp voice sounded like a nail scratching a board, and the stench of the alcohol on his breath turned her stomach. She pushed back the arm with a strength surprising herself.

"You know you want it," said the man.

She turned to face the persistent man. A bony-faced man with light hair looked back at her.

"I do?" she said crossly.

She could see the blood running through the throbbing vein on the man's neck. This was no innocent child; he was a man who had forced his hand around many girls' waists before.

She looked at the man's eyes and asked, "Do you want to get out of here?"

"Yep." The man followed her to the back porch.

Outside, her hand grabbed his and pulled it up to her lips.

"Ouch!" The man struggled to pull his hand back, but not before she let it go. He looked at his bloody punctured wrist and traces of blood on her lips.

"What are you? A vampire?"

ABOUT THE AUTHORS

Andrea Carter grew up in a small Southern California beach town. She teaches writing at Muir College at UC San Diego. She enjoys the beach, tries to practice surfing, and reads and writes mysteries.

Lina Karoline Castillo told other people's stories for thirty-plus years in public relations. Now, she tells her own stories: memories and moments from her life and those of her family—steeped in the carefree yet complex multicultural world she grew up in during the 1950s and '60s in Hawaii. When she's not in downward-facing dog, she's walking her dog on the beach in San Diego and Suquamish, Washington.

Tina Childers taught life skills to autistic teenage boys and horsemanship to Girl Scouts in the mountains of Julian before starting her career as an elementary educator. She is retired and resides in San Diego with her husband. She encounters leopard sharks and an occasional hammerhead during her La Jolla swims. When not traveling, she hikes Black Mountain with her faithful canine. She has two adult sons.

V.A. Christie is an author and artist from San Diego, California. Published by *The Write Launch, Brilliant Flash Fiction,* and *Atmosphere Press*, V.A. Christie was selected by Pen 2 Paper as a finalist in 2019. Follow V. A. Christie on twitter: https://twitter.com/VTheArtist and through Goodreads: https://www.goodreads.com/author/show/19720155.V_A_Christie.

Cornelia Feye is an author, art historian, and publisher. Born in Germany, she traveled around the world and lived in New York for five years, before settling in Ocean Beach, California. She published three art mystery novels. The first one, *Spring of Tears*, won the San Diego Book Award in 2011. The anthology *Magic, Mystery, & Murder*, co-edited with Tamara Merrill, won the San Diego Book Award in 2019. She is the founder of Konstellation Press, an indie publishing company for genre fiction and poetry. Her publications include art historical essays and reviews in English and German. www.konstellationpress.com

Max Feye is a writer plagued by the essential questions of life: How many pancakes can God eat? What happens after we die? What is dark matter? Most of all, is cereal considered a soup? After graduating from USC Film School, he moved to the great neon metropolis of Berlin, where he is part of a team that develops novels for a publishing company. He enjoys watching films, reading an eclectic array of books, meditating, and searching for the greatest falafel in Berlin.

Jennifer M. Franks is an author, mother, Navy wife, adventure traveler, animal lover, concert enthusiast, avid reader, and flamenco guitar player. She writes in genres that include travel memoir, fiction, and historical fiction. She currently lives in Coronado, California, with her family. In addition to writing, Jennifer is a co-founder of the Coronado Music Festival and board member of the Coronado Island Film Festival. Her novels include *Crown City by the Sea*, *The Lotus Blossom*, *Wild Card Willie and the Pony Express*, and *He Shall Be Peace*, and she has published a short story, *The Healing of the Paralytic*.

Valerie Hansen is a retired optometrist turned writer. She resides in San Diego, where she is quite tolerant of her neighbors and her relatives. She has published a novel with Konstellation Press: *Murder in the Wine Country—A Healdsburg Homicide*. She can be reached at HealdsburgHomicideSeries@gmail.com.

Suzanne Haworth has written for newspapers and magazines in the U.S. and abroad. She has worked as a carhop, croupier, museum docent, riding instructor, and secretary to an Australian ambassador. She made her way through university working for NASA at the Lawrence Radiation Laboratory. Marriage took her to Manhattan, Saudi Arabia, Indonesia, Sri Lanka, Singapore, and spots in between. This ex-pat finds settling in one place impossible and lives in La Jolla, California, and Naples, Florida.

Ladan Murphy is from Shiraz, Iran, city of poets, love, and reflection. She spent her childhood in pre-revolution Iran, where she developed her love for literature and poetry. When she is not at her day job as a software engineer, she sets aside her analytical side and writes picture books, science fiction, and fantasy stories.

Jennifer Pun is a Canadian film and television producer. She holds an MFA in Writing from Vermont College of Fine Arts. In her spare time, she devises zombie apocalypse survival strategies for her family.

Tabatha Tovar, MPH, is a writer, epidemiologist turned property manager, and mother of three children through birth and adoption. Her educational and occupational journey has given her opportunities to live and work in San Diego, San Francisco, New Orleans, and Gabon (West Africa). Her essay "Anika: Teaching Self Reliance" about raising a daughter with Down syndrome was published in *Fully Included—Stories to Inspire Inclusion* in 2018. Nowadays, she can be found hiking San Diego's canyons with her husband and children, laughing like a madwoman at a local standup comedy show, or cozy in a coffee shop transporting the worlds and characters in her head to her computer.

ALSO BY KONSTELLATION PRESS:

WWW.KONSTELLATIONPRESS.COM

- **Magic, Mystery & Murder**, anthology, edited by Cornelia Feye and Tamara Merrill
- **Spring of Tears,** Cornelia Feye
- **Private Universe,** Cornelia Feye
- **House of the Fox,** Cornelia Feye
- **Lessons in Disguise**, Kate Porter,
- **Family Myths,** Tamara Merrill
- **the wine tasted sweeter in the paper cups,** poems, Carlos Carrio
- **barefoot monks with sullied toes,** poems, Carlos Carrio
- **a tender force,** poems, Melissa Joseph
- **Captured Moments,** poems, Mary Kay Gardner
- **A Mouthful of Murder,** Andrea Carter
- **Murder in the Wine Country,** Valerie Hansen
- **Crown City by the Sea,** Jennifer M. Franks
- **Crossing Paths,** Susan Lewallen
- **The Cracks in the Life of Mike Anami,** Ted Shigematsu
- **Ballast Point Breakdown,** Corey Lynn Fayman